RANCOUR

A gripping murder mystery set on the west coast of Scotland

PETE BRASSETT

THE
BOOK
FOLKS

Paperback published by The Book Folks

London, 2018

© Pete Brassett

ISBN 978-1-7917-5561-4

www.thebookfolks.com

RANCOUR is the eighth novel by Pete Brassett to feature detectives Munro and West. Details about the other books can be found at the end of this one. All of these books can be enjoyed on their own, or as a series.

Prologue

For the hordes of hardened hillwalkers who relished the challenge of a gruelling six-mile hike culminating in a treacherous trek along a barely perceptible craggy path shrouded in low-lying cloud, the reward for completing the arduous ascent to the pinnacle of Goat Fell was a stunning view of Jura and Ben Lomond in the north and Ireland to the south. However, for the foolish few who attempted to conquer the snow-capped summit without the protection of suitable clothing, the aid of a map and a compass, the light of a torch, or the potentially life-saving connectivity of a mobile phone, the only reward was a one-way ticket to the promised land.

* * *

Unlike the majority of islanders who relied upon the lucrative seasonal tourist trade to swell the coffers, McIver's of Lamlash – with its corrugated iron roof and faded powder blue paintwork – derived its year-round income from maintaining everything from family saloons to row-crop tractors, and outboard motors to back-up generators, and functioned not just as a garage but as a community centre for talkative locals who, with scant regard for his workload, would often drop by unannounced for a strong brew and a wee chat with the convivial owner, John McIver.

As a first-rate mechanic, experienced climber, and volunteer with Arran mountain rescue, McIver thought nothing of downing tools and shutting-up shop in response to a callout which, during the hectic holiday season, was a regular occurrence with ninety percent of the hapless hikers being stretchered off the mountain in the bright, summer sunshine suffering from nothing more than a twisted ankle, a bruised ego, and some wounded pride. However, when the sound of his pager roused him from his slumber during the bleak winter nights, he knew the chances of finding anyone with a pulse were as slim as a playing card.

Packing a pocketful of his favourite whisky fudge, which he swore was more effective at bolstering faltering energy levels than any protein-packed cereal bar, McIver fired up the Land Cruiser and, squinting through the windscreen as the wipers cleared a swirling flurry of snow, headed for the base station in Brodick where he rallied with the rest of the team before commandeering the eight-wheel drive Argo Cat and heading up the hillside with his number two, the PE teacher from the high school, by his side.

At thirty-three years old, Isla Thomson – a svelte blonde with the physique of a marathon runner and a mind as agile as a double-jointed gymnast – could, much to the delight of her comrades, out-run, out-lift and out-smart almost any man; a not uncommon sight at the Pierhead Tavern on a Saturday night when any number of inebriated arm-wrestlers would summon her to a duel where the spoils for the victor, anything from a Bloody Mary to a plate of beer-battered haddock and chips, ensured she rarely reached for her purse.

'Alright, doll?' said McIver as the Argo crawled its way up the hillside. 'Where are we headed?'

'We're going to the Corrie side of the Goat Fell path,' said Thomson. 'The others are coming up the back.'

'And who are we looking for?'

'A young lass by the name of Ella MacCall. Apparently, she was with a group of four, the others turned back and she carried on alone.'

'Beggars belief,' said McIver. 'Does she have a phone?'

'No.'

'Numpty. I can't believe how utterly stupid folk can be.'

'I can.'

'Please don't tell me she's wearing a white, fur coat.'

'A bright, yellow anorak.'

'That's something. Did they raise 199?'

'Visibility's too low for the chopper, just now,' said Thomson, 'but they reckon it'll clear within the hour. Bailey's with the others. At least we can follow his nose if it's too dark for us to see.'

'That wee doggy, he never fails to surprise me. How the hell can he smell anything in this weather?'

'I like it,' said Thomson, 'it's bracing, it brings you alive.'

'Right enough,' said McIver, 'although I doubt this MacCall lassie would agree with you.'

Having travelled as far as the Argo would take them – where the snow-covered slopes gave way to gargantuan granite boulders – McIver and Thomson, clad in their red mountaineering jackets and guided by the light of their head lamps, set off on foot, clambering over the slippery rocks with their rucksacks on their backs and ropes slung across their shoulders, when the sound of a bark from across the ridge broke the eerie silence and drew them to a halt.

McIver hauled Thomson by the hand to a safe vantage point where they stood for a moment staring down at the motionless body, the snowy anorak glistening in the torchlight.

'God bless Bailey,' said McIver as they scrambled towards the frozen figure. 'Let's hope we're not too late.'

Judging by the four-inch gash to the side of the head, the dilated pupils and the dried, trickle of blood running from one corner of her mouth, it was clear that having sustained such an injury Ella MacCall would have been oblivious to the pain of her broken leg as she slipped in and out of consciousness, and might even have taken solace at the sight of the buzzards circling against a cloudy sky before succumbing to the cold as night descended.

McIver leaned over the body and brushed a lick of thick, brown hair from her forehead, knowing instinctively that the time for first aid had passed. He sighed and shook his head at the sight of her puffy, blue skin mottled with purple lesions, the blistered, chapped lips, and the swollen fingers, as rigid as a row of spent candles, blackened by frostbite.

'Poor lass,' said Thomson as she radioed for a stretcher. 'She's so young, too.'

'Aye,' said McIver, despondently. 'I have to say, if there's a downside to this job, Isla, then this is it.'

* * *

For the residents of Brodick the lure of the Ormidale Hotel lay not in the comfortable accommodation or the gut-busting breakfasts which left many a visitor reaching for the Rennie, but in the well-stocked bar, the Saturday night disco, and the charm of the proprietor, Kelly Baxter who, at 3:36 am, would rather have been sleeping than serving coffee to a punch-drunk constable in the public bar while he questioned three bedraggled tourists on the events leading up to the disappearance of their friend.

With all the guests accounted for, a perplexed Baxter hastened to the lobby, perturbed by the unexpected and somewhat ferocious banging at the door.

'Och, John, it's yourself,' she said. 'Isla, you too. Come in, come in. I'll fetch you both a drink.'

'Much obliged,' said McIver. 'Is Bobby here?'
'Aye, he's in the bar with the folk off the mountain.'

* * *

PC Bobby Mackenzie, one of only six officers stationed on the island, who was used to dealing with little more than the Saturday night drunks who, come daybreak, would invariably thank him for a night in the cells, was struggling to stay awake.

'John,' he said with a lethargic nod. 'I was going to call round in the morning.'

'It's morning now, so I've saved you a trip.'

'Did you find her?'

'Aye, we did,' said McIver as he addressed the group at the table. 'Are you the ones who were with her?'

The three girls, all in their late teens, bowed their heads and nodded in unison, intimidated by his hostile demeanour.

'How is she?' said Mackenzie.

'Dead.'

'Break it gently, why don't you.'

'She's dead, pal, there's no gentle way of putting it. You lot, how did you manage to make it down so quick?'

'Sorry,' said one of the girls. 'I'm not sure I understand.'

'It's a simple enough question. Jesus Christ, are you really that stupid? Look at you, you're dressed like you're away for a beer in Magaluf. Did you not consider what you were getting yourselves into, heading up the hill dressed like that?'

'But we didn't go,' said the girl. 'To the top, I mean.'

McIver glanced at Mackenzie, his blood boiling.

'What do you mean?' he said, menacingly. 'You didn't go?'

'We were too scared. We walked with Ella for about a mile, then we saw the cloud come down and we turned back.'

'But Ella carried on?'

'Aye. She was adamant.'

'And you didn't try to stop her?' said McIver. 'You let that wee lassie wearing next to nothing walk up there alone?'

The girls, rigid with fear, sat stock-still and stared sheepishly at the floor.

'And you call yourselves friends? By God, if you were my kids, I'd thrash the living…'

'That'll do, John,' said Mackenzie. 'Leave it to us, eh?'

'Are you joking me? A girl is dead because these so-called friends of hers couldn't be arsed to see her right.'

'I said I'll take care of it, okay?'

'No. It's not okay. Who made the call? Which one of you reported her missing?'

The girl on the left slowly raised her hand like a berated schoolchild owning up to a dishonest deed.

'I did,' she said.

'And why did you leave it so late to ring the police?'

'I don't know. We thought she'd be fine but then we got worried; worried she might have got herself into a wee bit of bother.'

'Well, you're not wrong there,' said McIver, raising his voice. 'Don't you realise we've been risking our lives because of your stupidity? Not just the two of us but the whole rescue team.'

'That's enough now, John,' said Mackenzie. 'You've had a hell of a night, you're tired, take yourself off and get some rest.'

'See here, Bobby, whether you like or not, these three are partly responsible for that lassie's death.'

'Maybe. And maybe not.'

'There's no maybe about it,' said McIver as he stormed from the room. 'I want them held to account, do you hear?'

Chapter 1

Unaware of the rumours surrounding her past – in particular the notion that as a young DS with the City of London police she'd enjoyed a hectic social life, a fancy apartment on Hoxton Square, and a reputation for being a hard-nosed detective – Charlotte West, contrary to popular belief, had in fact lived a life of solitude, returning home each evening to a cramped one bedroom flat on the Boundary Estate, which she'd shared with a bottle of Smirnoff, several takeaway menus, and a year's supply of sleeping tablets.

With no prospect of a promotion and a broken engagement to a philandering fiancé under her belt, she would – were it not for Munro's belief in her ability and his insistence that she join him north of the border – have no doubt been claiming unemployment benefit or manning the checkout at the local supermarket. Instead, she was heading-up a murder inquiry as a DI in the comparatively sedate surroundings of south-west Scotland where she'd expressed her gratitude by welcoming him as a house guest whilst his cottage in Carsethorn, subject to some lengthy renovation work, remained out of bounds.

However, it was not until her counsellor, coach, and confidant had moved out that she realised just how much she missed his companionship and his pithy observations on, amongst other things, her ability as a chef or how the reintroduction of national service and ducking-stools would lower the crime rate, and soon discovered that dining alone and spending her evenings binging on box-sets and Beaujolais was a depressing waste of time. As a result, she found herself rising unreasonably early to seek out the company she craved.

Wearing her black 501s and matching boots she walked the damp, dark streets to the HQ on King Street with her unruly hair tucked beneath a baker boy cap and her jacket zipped firmly against a biting wind blowing in off the Clyde.

* * *

With a mind like an algorithm, Detective Sergeant Dougal McCrae – whose pallid complexion and worsening eyesight were self-inflicted by-products of his affinity with technology and an aversion to daylight – sat swathed in the gloom of the office, his ghostly features illuminated by the glow of his computer screen, when the unexpected arrival of West caused him to jump in his seat.

'Flipping heck,' she said as she flicked the light switch. 'Did you forget to stick a shilling in the meter?'

'Sorry?' said Dougal, reeling from the glare.

'Never mind. You're too young.'

'Is this going to be a regular occurrence, miss?'

'Is what going to be a regular occurrence?'

'You. Upsetting the equilibrium by arriving so early.'

'Well, pardon me for being so diligent,' said West, tossing him a greasy, paper bag. 'Here you go, bacon and brown sauce. Fancy a cuppa?'

'Aye, cracking.'

'Good. Make me one while you're at it. No sign of Duncan?'

'No, no,' said Dougal. 'It's just the back of seven, give the man a chance. Is the boss not with you?'

'You mean Jimbo? Nah. He's back at his gaff in Carsethorn now that the builders have moved out, but he'll be here soon. You know what he's like, up with the larks.'

'Is it not a bit weird? Not having him around, I mean.'

'Yeah, a bit. But I'll get used to it. So, anything happening?'

'Aye, a few things,' said Dougal. 'We've a nutter on the loose with a machete.'

'Are you serious?'

'Deadly. He skelped some fella on Sandgate last night. Uniform have got their eyes open for the perp and I'm away to have a chat with the victim.'

'Blimey, did they find the weapon?'

'No, either the assailant hung on to it or he dumped it a few streets away. They're still looking.'

'What about cameras?' said West. 'Have you managed to track him?'

'We picked him up on one,' said Dougal, 'a slightly stocky fella, not too tall, but that's it for now.'

'Okay. What else?'

'You've got two cryptic messages to deal with.'

'Sounds intriguing.'

'There's a Post-it Note on your desk from DCI Elliot…'

'Crap.'

'…he wants a wee word. It's something to do with that Rona Macallan. He met with her solicitor last night.'

'But she was sent down weeks ago,' said West, 'and she's not coming out until she qualifies for her pension so why would he want a word about her?'

'I've no idea.'

'Sounds like trouble. What's the other thing?'

'A message from McLeod.'

'Our friendly forensic pathologist?'

'The same,' said Dougal. 'He finished a post-mortem on a young lassie just last night, a climbing accident apparently, but he says something's not right. He wants you to call him as soon as you can.'

'Okay,' said West as she crunched through her toastie. 'I'll polish this off and give him a bell while you stick the kettle on.'

* * *

As a rookie DC saddled with the more mundane tasks of an investigation, Duncan Reid was disappointed to discover that life in plain clothes did not include high-octane car chases, yelling at the top of his voice as he kicked down doors, or lurking in back alleys on the seedier side of town waiting for a tip-off from his favourite snitch. Nonetheless, he continued to hone his image as an undercover Caledonian crime-fighter by dressing like a stevedore from the glory days of the Clydeside shipyards with three days' worth of stubble on his face, a weather-beaten, brown leather jacket, and a woollen watch cap pulled down over his eyebrows.

'Good timing,' said West as he breezed through the door, a spent match dangling from his lower lip. 'Have you had your breakfast?'

'I have, miss. Aye.'

'Good. Don't bother sitting down, we're going out and you're driving.'

'No change there, then. Have you not got your car with you?'

'Nope. Flat battery.'

'Where are we headed?'

'The hospital. Our mate McLeod wants a chat and we need to get there soon, he's back up to Glasgow in a couple of hours.'

West paused at the sound of heavy, measured footsteps along the corridor, took a deep breath and braced herself for a confrontation with 'The Bear'.

'Off out, Charlie?' said DCI Elliot, beaming as his enormous bulk blocked the doorway.

'Afraid so, sir. You know what it's like: no rest for the wicked.'

'You too, Duncan?'

'Yes, indeedy. I'm driving.'

'The Figaro died,' said West, feigning a sense of urgency as she knocked back her tea and zipped her coat.

'Figaro? Now, that's a fine tune.'

'Is it?'

'Dear, dear, Charlie! The Barber of Seville! It's a shame James is not here, he'd put you right.'

'Maybe, but I think Sweeney Todd's more his style. Anyway, must dash, we've got a meeting with McLeod.'

'See me as soon as you're back. I need to talk to you about Rona Macallan.'

'Not bad news, is it?'

'No, no,' said Elliot. 'It's quite the opposite, Charlie. Quite the opposite.'

Chapter 2

Unlike those pessimistic pensioners who viewed retirement as the final furlong in the "Pearly Gates Longevity Stakes" rather than an inevitable consequence of the ageing process, James Munro – who thrived on the convoluted complexities of a criminal investigation – refused to replace his routine with the banality of daytime TV, spurned the notion of socialising with a gaggle of gormless seniors over a subsidised meal at the lunch club, and had yet to experience the joys of entering a room with no recollection as to why he was there. Instead, he embraced his position as a sagacious civilian volunteer with Police Scotland and, having purchased five litres of white gloss and a set of brushes, his role as a novice painter and decorator.

Relieved to see the back of the builders who'd all but acquired squatters' rights as they spent several weeks toiling for an average of twelve hours a day re-instating the rear portion of his house, which, as a consequence of a gas explosion by his own hand, had been blown to smithereens, Munro was overjoyed to be back in his own home and made a mental note to pen a letter of gratitude to the firm for restoring the rooms to their former glory in a style befitting the two-hundred-year-old cottage.

With the flagstones in the kitchen covered with dustsheets and the wall around the architrave neatly masked off – an enjoyably laborious task which had taken him the best part of an hour – he set about putting the finishing touches to the woodwork and stood poised brush in hand when, in accordance with Murphy's Law, the sound of his telephone caused his arm to jerk uncontrollably upwards resulting in a spatter of paint worthy of a Jackson Pollock.

'Munro!' he said, hollering down the phone. 'Who the devil is this?'

'It's Paul. Paul Jackson from The Steamboat. Have I interrupted something?'

'Hardly. I've not even started yet.'

'Started what?'

'Doesnae matter,' said Munro, 'but if you're ringing to drum up business for the raffle in that pub of yours, I'm telling you now, I cannae make it.'

'Why not?'

'Because with any luck I'll be watching some paint dry.'

'Well, it's not that, James,' said Jackson, quietly bemused, 'in fact, I was wanting to tap your brain about something. Something only you can help with.'

'Go on.'

'It's about Sophie.'

'Your daughter, Sophie?'

'Aye. I'm worried about her.'

'How so?'

'She was away up north, the night before last,' said Jackson, 'stopping with a friend of hers, Jess. Jess Sullivan. They were having a night out.'

'And?'

'I spoke to her when she arrived but I've not heard from since and she's not answering her phone. It's not like her.'

'Och, you know what youngsters are like,' said Munro, 'she probably had one too many and decided to…'

'She's seventeen, James. She doesn't drink. And she always calls.'

'Well, have you tried telephoning her friend? Did you not speak to the parents, at least?'

'I have,' said Jackson. 'They're not fussed, they reckon I'm over-reacting even though they've not heard from them either.'

'Damn and blast!' said Munro as the paint began dripping from the brush. 'See here, Paul, I'd like to help you out but I'm in the middle of a turpentine crisis, just now.'

'Turpentine?'

'Aye. I dinnae have any. Look, I'm retired now, you know that. Besides, this isn't my patch, hasn't been for years.'

'I know, but Kilmarnock is.'

'Kilmarnock?'

'Aye. That's where her friend stays,' said Jackson. 'They were off to The Palace Theatre. Look, I'm not one to impose, James, but if you could just tell me who I should be contacting about this, I can do it myself.'

Munro raised his eyes to the heavens and cursed under his breath as another drop of paint hit the floor.

'Listen,' he said, 'I'm away to Ayr soon enough, I'll drop by the pub on the way. I'll need her telephone number, a wee photo, and her friend's details. Got that?'

'I'm indebted to you James, much appreciated. There'll be a couple of pints waiting for you next time you're in.'

'It's not pints I'll be wanting. It's the Balvenie. Large ones, mind.'

Chapter 3

As a single mother of four from one of the less salubrious parts of town, where the most profitable business after the off-licence was the funeral parlour, the lady on reception – a smartly dressed sixty year old with a face like a bulldog and a devastating right hook – knew just how to handle the multitude of miscreants who approached her with aggressive demands to be treated for their alcohol-induced injuries, but one look at Duncan as he swaggered through the foyer like an armed robber short of a shotgun had her reaching below the desk, where her hand hovered nervously above the panic button.

'Alright, hen?' he said, his boyish grin putting her at ease. 'I'm Detective Constable Reid, and that there is DI West. Be a dear and buzz Doctor McLeod for me, would you? He's expecting us.'

West smiled as the willowy Andy McLeod, dressed in a crimson and black checked shirt and faded denim jeans, ambled towards her like a lightweight lumberjack, his bushy red beard the envy of Finnieston's hirsute hipsters.

'You should get out of scrubs more often,' she said coyly.

'That's not another invitation, is it, Charlotte?' said McLeod. 'Only as I recall, the last time we arranged something you blew me out.'

'I did not. I just got waylaid, work and stuff. You know how it is.'

'So, I'm in with a shout?'

'Maybe. If you buy a razor. Come on then, don't keep us in suspense. What's rattled your cage?'

'Let's have a seat,' said McLeod as he gestured towards an empty bench and pulled an iPad from his bag. 'This young lady is Miss Ella MacCall.'

West took the tablet and winced at the sight of the young girl's blotchy, blistered face.

'Blimey,' she said. 'And there was I thinking freezing was a means of preservation.'

'She was brought down off Goat Fell.'

'Goat who?'

'Goat Fell,' said McLeod. 'It's the tallest peak on Arran. Technically speaking, as it's less than three thousand feet, it's known as a Corbett.'

'Is it indeed. So basically, what you're saying is, she froze to death on the side a mountain, is that it?'

'Strictly speaking, yes.'

'I feel a "but" coming on.'

'But, as you know, my job's not simply to establish the cause of death but the means as well.'

'And you suspect foul play?'

'I do.'

'Are you saying she was murdered?' said Duncan.

'Aye. Well, maybe. Here's the thing, Constable. From what I gather she was with a group of friends, they turned back and this MacCall lassie continued up the fell alone. Of her own free will. So, under normal circumstances I'd classify her death as misadventure. However…'

McLeod took the iPad, swiped to technical specifications sheet, and handed it back.

'…I ran a few tests as a matter of course and found traces of a foreign substance.'

'You mean drugs?' said Duncan. 'Like what? Smack? Cocaine?'

'No, no. I'm afraid as far as you're concerned, it's worse than that. Much worse. Flunitrazepam. More commonly known as Rohypnol.'

'Rohypnol? Is that not the date-rape drug? Jeez-oh, are you telling me she was… on the mountain?'

'No, relax. There's no evidence of anything like that. My point is that had she not taken the Rohypnol, then the chances are she'd have made it down alive.'

'So you reckon someone gave it to her? Spiked her drink or something?'

'Must have,' said McLeod. 'Let's face it, it's not the kind of thing you'd take yourself, is it?'

'No, I suppose not. But why? Why would someone do that, especially if she was off up the hill?'

'I'd love to help but that's not a question I can answer,' said McLeod. 'I've done my bit.'

'You certainly have,' said West. 'Can you send me a full report?'

'I already have.'

'Anything else we should know about?'

'No, that's it. The lads on Arran should be in touch soon enough, you can liaise with them. The investigating officer is a fella by the name of Mackenzie. Right, that's me back to Glasgow. I've work to do.'

'When are you down next?' said West as he stood to leave.

'I'm not really sure. It all depends on what, or should I say, who, turns up. Why?'

'No reason. Thought you might like to go out, that's all.'

McLeod cocked his head and smiled.

'Aye,' he said. 'I'd like that. Is it a wee bar you have in mind? Or a restaurant, maybe?'

'Actually,' said West, 'I was thinking barber shop. Give me a call.'

* * *

Whilst confident in his ability to resolve any conundrum concerning the who-did-what-to-whom-and-why, Dougal was not given to brazen displays of riddle-solving and consequently squirmed under the perpetual gaze of a bored, larger than life senior officer who, in an effort to soften his reputation as a grizzly, had struck up a somewhat dreary conversation concerning his wife's recipes while he waited for West to return.

'So,' he said, 'what's it to be? Tagliatelle or spaghetti?'

'Sorry?'

'Carbonara, man!' said Elliot. 'I asked you what we should be using in a carbonara! You see, Dougal, Mrs Elliot is making her carbonara tonight and I have to say it's really not bad, not bad at all. Double cream, garlic, smoked ham...'

'Sounds smashing.'

'...it is, but she will insist on using tagliatelle and I say it should be spaghetti. So, you tell me, am I right or am I wrong?'

With his knowledge of Italian cuisine limited to pizza, tinned ravioli, and supermarket ready meals, Dougal surreptitiously turned to the internet for guidance.

'Well,' he said, speaking with the conviction of a Neapolitan native, 'if it's a traditional carbonara you're after, then it should be spaghetti, but you could use linguine instead.'

'I knew it!' bellowed Elliot. 'Spaghetti! I'd best telephone her now before she heads to the shops.'

'And no cream.'

'What's that?'

'Cream. There's no cream in a real carbonara,' said Dougal. 'Nor is there any garlic. Or ham. It should be guanciale.'

Elliot sat back and pondered for a moment.

'I think I'll keep that wee nugget of information to myself. I'll not take it without the cream.'

'Cream?' said West as she blew through the door. 'It's too bleeding cold for cream, it's gravy weather. In fact, it's pie, mash and gravy weather. And I'm starving.'

'Charlie, I'm glad you're back. I need a word.'

'Can we have lunch first?'

'You cannot,' said Elliot. 'Have yourself a seat. First of all, there's been an incident on Arran.'

'Don't tell me,' said West as she placed her forefingers on her temples and closed her eyes. 'I'm seeing a young girl, she's on a mountain and she's…'

'Dear God! That's uncanny! How on earth…'

'We just saw McLeod. He filled us in.'

'I see,' said Elliot, clearing his throat. 'You nearly had me there, Charlie. Nearly, but not quite. Young Dougal here has all the information you need. The rest of the group are still on the island but they're leaving tomorrow so you'd best get yourselves on a ferry just as soon as you can.'

'In this weather?' said West. 'That's great. Why don't we go white-water rafting while we're at it?'

'I hope you're not including me on this trip,' said Duncan. 'Only me and boats, we're not a good combination. Besides, I'm not sure the Audi will make it, it's due a service.'

'Which brings me to my next point,' said Elliot. 'Rona Macallan.'

'Here we go,' said West as she slumped in a seat. 'So, what's up? Has something hit the fan? Has she appealed?'

'No, no. She's simply made a few arrangements concerning her domestic affairs, that's all.'

'I don't follow.'

'Well, for example, the fella up the road will be looking after her livestock…'

'The goats and the chickens and the horses. We know that.'

'…and a friend of hers will be house-sitting until, well, until she's released, I imagine.'

'No offence, sir, but what has any of this got to do with us?'

'Not us, Charlie. You.'

'Me?'

'Aye,' said Elliot. 'You see, she's instructed her solicitor to off-load some of her belongings, those she feels will be worthless on her return to society.'

'Like what?'

'Well, there's a trailer and a quad bike for starters. And then there's a Land Rover Defender which, I'm reliably informed, she offered to you when you arrested her.'

'Yeah, she did,' said West, 'but I thought, you know protocol and stuff, I didn't think I was allowed to have it.'

'Quite right, Charlie, but now that we're done with it and she's away for the foreseeable, circumstances have changed. She still wants you to have first refusal. If you're not interested, it will go to auction.'

'Not if I can help it,' said West. 'Nice one, sir. Cheers. What's his number? I'll give him a bell right now.'

'I'd not do that if I were you.'

'Why not?'

'Because,' said Elliot, 'he's downstairs in the pound. He's checking the SOCOs didn't cause any damage when they pulled it apart. If I'm not mistaken, he's got the logbook with him too.'

'You've landed on your feet there, miss,' said Dougal. 'You'll not go wrong with a Defender, not up here.'

'Right enough,' said Duncan. 'And now that you've got your own set of wheels, you'll not be needing me to drive; so that's me off the hook.'

'In your dreams,' said West. 'You're still coming with me.'

'Oh, is it not Dougal's turn to go? The last time I jumped a ferry with you it almost turned into a submarine.'

'Stop whingeing and get your act together.'

'I'll leave you to it,' said Elliot as he left the room. 'I need a wee chat with my pasta chef. Keep me informed of your progress.'

* * *

Elated about her impending acquisition, West zipped her jacket and turned for the door.

'I'm nipping downstairs,' she said. 'Dougal, favour please. Can you check the ferry times for…'

'Already sorted, miss. Next one's at three-twenty which gets you in at four-fifteen. I'd not leave it later than that if I were you.'

'You're too efficient for your own good, you know that? I don't suppose you've…'

'I have, aye. I've managed to get you into the Ormidale in Brodick, it's a hop and a skip from the ferry terminal and it's where the girls are staying. I've booked two rooms, all paid for and the reservation's in your name.'

'You mean we're not coming back tonight?' said Duncan.

'Might not be coming back at all,' said West. 'You know what the sea's like at this time of year – all choppy and stuff. One big swell and that could be us gone forever.'

'Thanks very much, miss. Thanks very much indeed. I'm away to fetch some Kwells. Back in a tick.'

'Oh Dougal,' said West, 'have you heard from Jimbo? It's not like him to be this late.'

'I have indeed, miss. He said he had something to attend to at home and wasn't sure what time he'd be in.'

'Volunteers, eh? Just because they don't get paid, they think they can do what they like.'

Chapter 4

Throughout the course of his illustrious career, when it came to making snap decisions – be it a life-saving manoeuvre in the presence of an armed suspect or assessing the culpability of a defendant in the stark surroundings of the interview room – Munro invariably relied upon his infallible instinct to provide a favourable outcome. So, when faced with a choice between enjoying the comfort of a wood-burning stove, a strong cup of tea and a few fingers of shortbread whilst applying a coat of paint to the door frame or heading out into a wind chill of minus six for a few hours of unpaid work it was, as West would say, a no-brainer.

Cursing as a violent gust of wind whipped what was left of his thinning grey hair into a less than flattering comb-over, he sped towards to The Steamboat, collected the contact details for the landlord's wayward daughter, and continued on his way beset with a determination to cover the seventy miles to Ayr in under an hour.

Settling back, he braced his arms against the wheel and floored the ageing Peugeot, his dour demeanour deepening as he flew by the muddy, fallow fields flanking the deserted road overshadowed by a raft of puffy, snow-laden clouds tumbling across a murky, grey sky.

Precisely fifty-two minutes later – an unverifiable and somewhat dubious fact based on the inability of his watch to maintain a semblance of accurate timekeeping – he arrived at the office, hesitated, and pulled a folded sheet of A4 from his pocket.

'They'll not miss me for an hour,' he muttered as he pulled away. 'They'll not miss me at all.'

* * *

The house on Woodstock Street, an unassuming traditional semi with a slate roof and a vast gravel drive, was no different to the other family homes on the quiet residential road set away from the hubbub of Kilmarnock's town centre.

Wishing he'd worn a hat as the first few drops of ice-cold rain spattered the top his head, he knocked the door, stepped back, and stood with his hands clasped firmly behind his back.

'Apologies for disturbing you,' he said with a genial smile. 'I'm enquiring after a Miss Jessica Sullivan, I believe she lives here.'

A smartly dressed woman in navy blue slacks and a white blouse, her otherwise stylish appearance let down by a pair of lurid, pink slippers and enough red lipstick to coat a Ferrari, folded her arms and scowled suspiciously at Munro.

'And why,' she said, 'would an old fella like yourself be asking after my daughter?'

'Forgive me. The name's Munro. James Munro. I'm a friend of Paul Jackson, he owns the pub in Carsethorn and his daughter, Sophie…'

'Oh, Sophie! You should've said. Nice wee girl. Very polite.'

'Indeed she is,' said Munro. 'The thing is, Mrs Sullivan, Paul's not heard from Sophie since she arrived here and he's concerned for her welfare.'

'I know. I spoke to him on the telephone. He near enough took my head off, yelling like I'm the world's worst babysitter.'

'Och, he's just worried,' said Munro. 'I understand Sophie and your daughter were on a night out, is that correct?'

'It is,' said Sullivan, 'but what's it got to do with you?'

Munro pulled a handkerchief from his pocket and dabbed a drop of rain from the tip of his nose.

'I've known Paul for many years,' he said, 'and as a police officer, a retired police officer I should say, I've offered to make some enquiries on his behalf.'

'That's very neighbourly of you,' said Sullivan, 'but there's a lot of folk round here pretending to be somebody they're not. Have you got any ID?'

'If, by ID, you mean a warrant card, then the answer is no. But I do have a security pass, a driving licence, and a loyalty card for my local supermarket.'

Sullivan leaned against the door and smiled.

'You're quite funny, you know that?'

'I hope not,' said Munro. 'That would never do. See here, Mrs Sullivan, I quite understand your apprehension in discussing Jessica with a stranger. If it helps, I can give you the telephone number of Detective Inspector West, she's…'

'No, you're alright,' said Sullivan. 'I believe you, but I don't see how I can help. You should tell Sophie's dad he worries too much.'

'Is that so?'

'It is, aye. Look, they're not wee girls anymore, they're grown women. They can look after themselves.'

'Sophie's not yet eighteen, Mrs Sullivan. I'm afraid I have to side with her father on this one.'

'That's me told.'

'So, your daughter Jessica, does she make a habit of stopping out without telling you?'

'She does. It's no big deal, Mr Munro. I trust her implicitly.'

'But you've not heard from her yet?'

'Not yet.'

'Okay, back to last night. They went to the Palace Theatre, is that correct?'

'Aye,' said Sullivan. 'Alabama 3.'

'I'm sorry?'

'They're a band. Jessica says they're pure brilliant.'

'Does she, indeed! And what time did they leave?'

'Six, six-thirty, I think.'

'And was it just the two of them? I mean, were they meeting anybody else? Some other friends, perhaps?'

'No, no. Just them.'

'And can you tell me what they were wearing?'

'Now you're asking,' said Sullivan, 'hold on now, Jessica was in her favourite ripped jeans, a paisley print top and a denim jacket.'

'And Sophie?'

'The usual. Like a nun on her day off. A full-length flowery thing and a big overcoat. Oh, and a knitted beanie-type hat on her head.'

'And after the show,' said Munro, 'have you any idea where they might have gone after the show?'

'Who knows. A few drinks, a club, or maybe they got lucky and met a couple of fellas.'

'Aye, maybe,' said Munro, despairing at her approach to parenting. 'I appreciate your time, Mrs Sullivan, and listen, if you should hear from either of them, then telephone Paul and put him out of his misery.'

Munro returned to the car and pulled a shabby, black baseball cap from the debris littering the boot before embarking on the short stroll to the Palace Theatre where, pausing briefly to admire the red sandstone building and its impressive Italianate tower, he pondered why, given its proximity to Woodstock Street, the girls had failed to return home.

'Alright pal,' said a young man pinning a poster to the wall of the foyer. 'If it's the Grand Hall you're after, it's next door.'

'No, no,' said Munro, 'it's the theatre I want.'

'Sorry but we're closed just now and we've nothing on tonight anyway.'

'Nae bother. It's last night I'm interested in.'

'Well, leave your number. If we ever decide to do an H. G. Wells season, I'll let you know when we're showing *The Time Machine*.'

'Very good,' said Munro. 'That was almost funny. The Alabama 3, they were playing last night, were they not?'

'They were indeed, and a good gig it was too, by all accounts. To be honest, I'm surprised it didn't sell out. So, what were you after? Some merchandise is it? A T-shirt or a CD or something?'

'Not quite. The name's Munro. I'm making enquiries about a young girl who's gone missing.'

'Police?'

'Retired.'

'Once a copper, as they say. Listen, if a wee lassie's in danger then I'm happy to help, within reason, of course.'

'Of course,' said Munro, 'I'm much obliged Mr...?'

'Ian. Ian will do.'

'As you wish. I notice you've no cameras outside, Ian. Is that not a bit remiss?'

'No, it's a quiet place, this. Besides, the building's listed, I'm not sure they'd get permission for it.'

'Fair enough.'

'But we've a few inside,' said Ian pointing to the ceiling above the desk. 'There's one right there. We clock everyone as they come in and again as they leave, just in case.'

'Then that's exactly what I'd like to see,' said Munro. 'The lassie in question was coming to the concert and I want to be sure that she actually arrived.'

'No bother!' said Ian. 'Come with me and I'll set you up. It'll not take long. Doors open an hour before the performance and there's no entry for latecomers, they have to wait for the interval.'

The large split-screen monitor displaying real-time images of the foyer, the café-bar, the fire exits, and the entrance to the restrooms was seemingly the only nod to modern technology in an otherwise dated office with a dry wipe board listing forthcoming events leaning against the wall, boxes of flyers strewn across the floor, and a desk doubling as the lost property department obscured by a pile of coats.

'Pull up a chair if you can find one,' said Ian. 'Okay, we're off.'

Munro, choosing to stand, pulled his spectacles from his breast pocket and watched closely as the screen filled with the image of a young man with his back to the camera fumbling with a set of keys.

'That's me opening up,' said Ian. 'Right, will I leave you to it, then?'

'No, actually, if I'm not keeping you from your work then I could do with the company. Two sets of eyes are better than one and you know how to make this thing go back and forth, should I need it to.'

'Right you are. So, who are we looking for?'

'Two girls, pals together,' said Munro. 'Both about five-six, one in a denim jacket and torn jeans, the other in an overcoat and a woolly hat.'

Ian settled into his seat and crossed his legs whilst Munro, intent on missing nothing, leaned into the screen and scrutinised every single person in the queue, growing increasingly despondent at the lack of lone females.

'It's mainly couples,' he said, 'and single men. Do the chaps in the band not have hordes of screaming lassies chasing them with proposals of marriage?'

'I wouldn't know,' said Ian, 'I'm more a John Denver man myself.'

'You surprise me.'

'How so?'

'Well, a young lad like yourself, I'd have thought…'

'I can't stand noise, Mr Munro. I like things nice and quiet.'

'You and me both, son. You and me both. Is that it?'

'Aye. Unless you want to see them all come out again.'

'Not necessary,' said Munro. 'I think I've seen enough.'

'Perhaps they got delayed and missed the doors?'

'I doubt it. They're a ten-minute walk away.'

'Will we check the footage from the bar?' said Ian. 'Perhaps they had a few drinks beforehand and thought sod the band, we'll have a few more.'

'Would they have used the same entrance to reach the bar?'

'They would indeed.'

'Then no. What about tickets?' said Munro. 'Would they have bought them here? From the box office?'

'Aye, maybe, or off the website. If they used a credit card in their names then I could check for you…'

'If it's not too much trouble.'

'…but they may have got them through the online agency. We're registered with Skiddle.'

'Either way,' said Munro with a sigh, 'tickets aside, the fact remains they didnae show.'

'Sorry, I'm not sure what else I can do.'

'You've done quite enough. And I thank you for that.'

'Anytime. Well, good luck. I hope you find them.'

'So do I,' said Munro. 'So do I.'

* * *

As the sky darkened and the temperature dipped, the rain now falling as sleet and bolstered by a biting south-westerly wind, battered Munro's back as he pulled his phone from his pocket and called the office.

'Dougal,' he said, raising his voice against the traffic trundling through the slush. 'Is Charlie there?'

'Alright, boss? No, she's left already.'

'Left?'

'Aye, she and Duncan, they're away to Arran.'

'Anything interesting?'

'Lassie on Goat Fell. She didn't make it down.'

'Dear, dear, that's too bad,' said Munro. 'A tragedy in fact. Aye, that's the word, a tragedy. How about you? Are you busy just now?'

'I have to see a fella about a machete.'

'This had better be good.'

'He ran into one last night,' said Dougal. 'I'm away to see if he's any idea who was holding it. Why, are you wanting something?'

'Unofficially, Dougal, I am. Listen, if you have the time, would you mind tracing some ticket sales for me? A band calling themselves the Alabama 3. They played the Palace in Kilmarnock last night.'

'Right you are, boss, can you make it any easier?'

'I can indeed. The only agency that the theatre's registered with is a company called Skiddle. I need to know if anyone by the name of Sullivan or Jackson purchased tickets through them for the show.'

'No bother, boss. I'll be an hour, I'll see what I can find out as soon as I get back.'

* * *

Unlike a minority of teens who regarded full-time employment as a drain on their valuable leisure time and parents as an interest-free source of income, Sophie Jackson – a timid, well-educated young lady with aspirations of joining the teaching profession – was raised on blood, sweat and tears and a respect for her elders. Deferring the inevitable call to her father, a frustrated Munro pulled his cap low over his brow and headed for the police office on St Marnock Street.

As most visitors to the station arrived via the back door with nothing to look forward to but a formal charge of anti-social behaviour, possession, or more commonly, aggravated assault, it was – for the burly constable bursting at the seams of his black shirt – a refreshing change to greet somebody at the front desk.

'Afternoon, sir,' he said with an enthusiastic grin. 'How are you?'

'Not good,' said Munro. 'Truth be known, I've been better.'

'It's probably the weather, it has that effect on everyone. So, what can I help you with?'

'I want to report a missing person.'

'Oh aye? Get away, did they?'

'Did who get away?'

'The fella you apprehended.'

'You've lost me.'

'I'm just assuming that if a police officer wanders in here to report a missing person, then he must have...'

'Jumping Jehoshaphat! What makes you think I'm a police officer?'

'Something to do with the word *police* on your cap?'

Munro raised his eyes and allowed himself a wry smirk.

'Och, it's been a while since I've worn one of these,' he said. 'I clean forgot. The name's Munro. James...'

'Are you joking me?'

'And why would I do that?'

'No, seriously,' said the constable. 'DI Munro?'

'The same.'

'Your reputation, as they say, precedes you.'

'Then you'll know not to play the fool with me. Am I right?'

'Sir.'

'Good. Now that we understand each other, perhaps we can get on. I, that is to say, my good friend Mr Jackson, is concerned for the safety of his daughter. She's not made contact for nearly forty-eight hours and that, to coin a phrase, is out of character.'

'Okay,' said the constable. 'Let's start with the name then we'll get some details.'

'Jackson. Miss Sophie Jackson of The Steamboat Inn, Carsethorn.'

The constable, wary of overstepping the mark, glanced furtively at Munro and paused as if daring himself to ask the question.

'Young lass?' he said. 'Blondish hair, five-five, five-six?'

'Aye. How did you...'

'Just give me a moment, would you please,' said the constable as he disappeared through the back door. 'I'll be right back.'

'Where the devil are you...?'

'Two minutes, sir! I swear, two minutes.'

Agitated by the constable's vanishing act, Munro removed his cap and ran his fingers through his hair, ready to explode like a boxful of bangers when a different officer of a senior rank came through the door.

'DI Munro?' he said.

'It's Mr Munro! I'm retired!'

'All the same, it's a pleasure to meet you. Sergeant Ryan, I've heard a lot about...'

'Stop havering, laddie! What's going on here?'

'I think we've got the girl you're looking for.'

* * *

With all the rooms occupied and latecomers being forced to wait in the back of a Black Maria, the custody suite – as busy as a highland hotel on Hogmanay – was filled with the muffled cries of largely inebriated teenagers protesting their innocence amidst claims of police brutality.

Munro took a few steps forward and peered through the viewing hatch of Detention Cell One where Sophie Jackson, looking tired but otherwise none the worse for wear, was lying on the bunk with her eyes closed and her knees pulled to her chest.

'That's her,' he said, his shoulders slumping with relief. 'How has she been?'

'Quiet,' said Ryan. 'She's not said a word to anyone about anything.'

'But she did give her name?'

'Aye, but that's about all she gave. After that she clammed up. She's not moved from that position since we brought her in.'

'And when was that?'

'Early hours,' said Ryan. 'Around 2:00 am, I think.'

'2:00 am? Good grief man, that's more than twelve hours ago! What the blazes have you been doing all this time?'

'Well, apart from keeping an eye on her, we've been telephoning every single Jackson in Kilmarnock and…'

'Kilmarnock!' bellowed Munro. 'If you'd looked in her purse or checked her phone, you'd know she lives in Carsethorn!'

'With all due respect, sir,' said Ryan bluntly. 'She's not carrying a purse. Or a phone.'

* * *

Best described as green, naïve, or at the very least, ingenuous, Sophie Jackson – trusting to a fault – would think nothing of leaving her handbag unattended, lending her phone to a total stranger or, despite the proliferation of undesirables in the area, walking the shady streets of an unfamiliar neighbourhood with only her wits to guide her.

Fearing she'd fallen prey to a track-suited ned off his face on super strength cider, Munro glared at the sergeant with a look of consternation on his face.

'Where did you find her?' he said.

'Up on Fowlds Street, sir. Not far from Bakers. She was half asleep, slumped on the pavement.'

'Bakers?'

'Aye, it's a nightclub.'

'And this club,' said Munro, 'does it have a reputation for trouble?'

'Actually no. It draws a decent crowd, generally well-behaved. We figured Miss Jackson had probably been enjoying herself a bit too much, if you know what I mean.'

'So, what's the story? Did somebody report her as drunk and disorderly?'

'No, no,' said Ryan, 'nothing like that. We had a report of a disturbance as the club was kicking out.'

'A brawl?'

'Not quite. Seems some fella was trying to bundle off a couple of lassies into the back of his motor. One ran off but a witness says the other one got in. She assumed it was her boyfriend, or a taxi.'

'And was it a taxi?'

'No, we've checked. It's silver Vauxhall Insignia, privately owned. We've run the index through the DVLA and the lads are on it now.'

'And this girl, the one who jumped in, did you get a description?'

'We did,' said Ryan, 'but it's vague. Black jeans. Denim jacket.'

'And the one who ran off?'

'That was Miss Jackson.'

Munro clasped his hands behind his back, walked slowly to the cell and took another peek at Sophie before returning to Ryan.

'And the doctor,' he said. 'He's given her the all-clear?'

'Sorry?'

'The medical examiner. Are you telling me she's not been checked over?'

'No, I mean, at least I don't...'

'Get him now, you blithering fool! If she's been assaulted or drugged, you're wasting valuable time!'

'Sir.'

'And open the blasted door, I need to speak with her. Now!'

* * *

Munro gently closed the door behind him, unzipped his jacket and squatted beside the bed.

'Sophie,' he said, almost whispering. 'Sophie, it's James, from up the way. Can you hear me?'

Sophie, as if roused from a pleasant dream, opened her eyes, blinked as she tried to focus, and smiled.

'Hello, Mr Munro,' she said. 'What are you doing here?'

'Och, I was just passing, thought I'd pop in. How are you feeling?'

'Tired. My head's mince.'

'I'm not surprised. That was some night you had from what I hear.'

'That's what worries me,' said Sophie, her docile expression turning to one of angst. 'I'm not one for the drink, Mr Munro, you know that.'

'I do indeed. Listen, if you're up to talking we can have a wee chat, if not, I'll leave you be and come back later.'

'No, you're alright,' said Sophie, sitting up. 'It might help.'

'Good girl. So, first things first, are you needing anything? Some water? A cup of tea? Something to eat perhaps?'

'No. I'm fine.'

'Okey-dokey,' said Munro, 'in that case, let's crack on. Now, here's the thing, once we're done here, I've asked a doctor to come by and give you the once over, just to make sure you didnae take a wee bump to the head. He'll also take a blood sample, are you okay with that?'

'Aye, I suppose so, but why does he need a blood sample?'

'Nothing to worry about, it's just a precaution. Now then, obviously you didnae have anything to drink last night?'

'No, just orange juice.'

'And you were feeling…?'

'Aye, I was feeling okay, I think. Then we had one more drink before we left.'

'We?'

'Me and Jess.'

'And then?'

'That's just it,' said Sophie. 'There is no then. The next thing I remember is waking up here. I'm scared, Mr Munro, did I do something wrong? Have they arrested me? Because if they have…'

'Calm down,' said Munro, raising his hand with a reassuring smile, 'you've not been arrested and you've done nothing wrong. We just need to find out happened.'

'What about Jess?'

'Och, she's probably home, tucked up in bed. Look, I'll give her folks a wee call in a moment, then I'll telephone your father and let him know we're on our way. Just a couple of more questions first. Tell me, you and Jess, did you happen to meet any lads along the way?'

'No. Not that I recall.'

'So, nobody tried to chat you up or offer to buy you a drink?'

Sophie shook her head and frowned.

'No,' she said. 'I think Jess was chatting to someone when we left but I'm really not sure.'

'Dinnae worry. Okay, last question, your father says that you and Jess were off to see a band at the Palace Theatre. Did you not go?'

Sophie, her cheeks flushing, bowed her head.

'No,' she said shamefully. 'I'm so sorry, Mr Munro, really I am. Jess made it up, she said it would be a good cover for me. Her mum's not bothered what she does but if my Dad…'

'It's not worth fretting about,' said Munro. 'Let's just say, least said, soonest mended.'

Munro gently closed the door and beckoned the doctor to one side.

'Take a blood sample,' he said as he handed him a business card. 'I need you to check for Benzodiazepines as quick as you can. Send the results here for the attention of DI West, and this is my number on the back. You're to call me as soon as you have the results. Do I make myself clear?'

Chapter 5

Being battered by a cyclonic westerly blowing a gale force nine was, for the crew of the *Caledonian Isles,* just another day at the office but for Duncan – who'd earned his sea legs aboard a pedalo on the placid waters of a boating lake in Girvan – it was a test of faith over endurance.

Keen to avoid the view from the window, which changed rhythmically from that of a leaden sky to a harrowing scene of six-foot swells, he sat cowering in his seat as the ferry pitched and yawed its way doggedly across the Firth of Clyde before finally lumbering into port forty-five minutes later than scheduled and spilling its cargo of pasty-faced passengers onto the dockside, each keen to sample the delights of Brodick's nearest pub as a matter of some urgency.

Assuming his bravado had jumped ship shortly after leaving the mainland, West – smirking slyly at his malaise – fired up the Land Rover and sped towards the hotel keen to interview the friends of Ella MacCall as soon as possible, thereby leaving the rest of the evening free to fill her face over a glass or two of Arran's Lochranza Reserve.

Set in seven acres of mature woodland with all the charm of a Victorian manor house, The Ormidale Hotel –

despite the inclement weather – was full to overflowing with locals sniggering into their pints at the tourists' inability to cope with a wee breeze and a flurry or two.

Kelly Baxter, as affable as ever, took one look at Duncan, poured a glass of tonic water, and slid it across the bar with a couple of aspirin.

'Something you ate?' she said, winking at West.

'Aye,' said Duncan. 'More than likely. We've a couple of rooms in the name of West.'

'Detective Inspector West?'

'That's us.'

'So, it's Bobby you'll be wanting?'

'Constable Mackenzie?'

'He's waiting for you out the back, it's a nice wee room so you'll have plenty of privacy.'

'And the girls?' said West.

'They're upstairs.'

'Any idea when they're leaving?'

'Tomorrow morning,' said Baxter. 'Their ferry leaves just after eleven o'clock, assuming the weather doesn't take a turn for the worse.'

West spun on her heels as a customer snatched a plate from the bar loaded with a homemade steak and kidney pie and vanished into the crowd.

'Tell you what,' she said, 'there's nothing like a boat trip to work up an appetite.'

'If you say so,' said Duncan.

'Oh, come on, if it was all plain sailing, it wouldn't be fun, would it? It wasn't that bad, just a bit choppy, that's all.'

'No offence, miss, but I've been held captive for half an hour by a madwoman behind the wheel of a car with no heating and dodgy wipers who obviously passed her test at a demolition derby, then, after twenty years of being an atheist, I finally found God and made my peace before we all ended up like a tin of sardines at the bottom of the ocean. So, with all due respect, aye, it was that bad, and now that we're back on terra firma I'm in need of a stiff drink. Can I get you one?'

'Not yet,' said West, grinning, 'we need to have a chat with Mackenzie first, and then the girls.'

'Are you joking me?' said Duncan. 'Not even a small one? A wee dram? For medicinal purposes?'

'Nope. Come on, we've got work to do.'

'Och, I never realised you were such a hard taskmaster.'

'Sorry?'

'I said, it's only a Talisker I'm after.'

* * *

Apart from his training at the police college in Kincardine and a two-year probationary period spent honing his skills with the residents and sightseers of neighbouring Campbeltown on the Kintyre peninsula, native islander Bobby Mackenzie, despite his years, had never left home.

Clad in his yellow hi-vis jacket cradling a lukewarm mug of tea, he glanced up as Duncan entered the room, his face breaking into a sea of weather-beaten wrinkles.

'Are you okay?'

'Aye,' said Duncan, scowling. 'Why wouldn't I be?'

'No reason. It's just that you look, well, a wee bit…'

'I'm fine pal. It's just a touch of indigestion, that's all.'

Mackenzie stood and proffered his hand.

'PC Mackenzie,' he said. 'You must be…'

'No. I'm not. I'm DC Reid. And this is DI West.'

'Don't look so surprised,' said West as she slung her coat over the back of a chair. 'Apart from being skilled in the art of washing-up, I can also cook, drive a car, and probably drink you under the table. Oh, and I'm quite good solving the odd crime too.'

'Sorry, miss. I didn't mean…'

'Forget it. Now, let's push on. Ella MacCall. From the top.'

'Well there's not much to tell really. In fact, if you don't mind me saying so, I'm not really sure why you're here, I mean, was it not just a climbing accident?'

'Nope, afraid not,' said West as she pulled up a chair. 'The poor girl was drugged.'

'Drugged? Are you sure?'

'If you want to question the professional findings of the pathologist, Constable Mackenzie, then maybe I should let you lead the investigation.'

'No, no. Sorry. It's just, well it's just a shock, that's all. I mean, drugged? Here? I think you should have a word with McIver. That's John McIver, he led the team who brought her down.'

'We will,' said West. 'Later. Now, let's try again, shall we?'

Mackenzie lowered his eyes, flicked open his notebook, and cleared his throat.

'Okay,' he said, 'we have four girls on a wee break. A Miss Holly Paterson, Miss Kirsty Young, a Megan Dalgleish, and of course, Ella MacCall. They all travelled together from Irvine and arrived on the 6:55 from Ardrossan. Their rooms were booked in advance. After checking in they had supper here at the hotel and then a walk around the town before going to bed. The following day they had breakfast, walked up to the Co-op, to fetch provisions I imagine, then retired to their rooms. They set off again around lunchtime.'

'Set off where?' said Duncan.

'Why, Goat Fell of course.'

'Was it not a bit late to be heading up there? I mean, they'd have only had four hours of daylight left, five at best.'

'Aye, right enough,' said Mackenzie, 'but if no-one knew where they were going, then no-one could stop them.'

'Okay,' said West, 'apart from their crap sense of timing, was there anything suspicious about them when they arrived? Were they skittish? Edgy? Quiet? Withdrawn?'

'No, quite the opposite, quite an exuberant bunch by all accounts. Easy going. The only thing that stood out was their clothing, not exactly dressed for the time of year, let alone taking a walk up a mountain.'

'How so?' said Duncan.

'Kagools, T-shirts, trainers.'

'So it could have been an impulsive thing,' said West, 'to climb Goat Fell. A spur of the moment decision not really knowing what they were letting themselves in for.'

'Aye, maybe,' said Mackenzie, 'but to be honest miss, they'd have to have had a screw loose to try it. Let's face it, it's not as if they're from California, they know what the weather's like.'

West leaned back, folded her arms and stared at the cobwebs hanging from the light fitting on the ceiling.

'Did they hook up with anyone here?' she said. 'At the hotel, in the bar? Did they get friendly with anyone in particular?'

'Not that I'm aware of, and I have asked. Pretty much kept themselves to themselves.'

'Okay, so they set off at lunchtime. What next?'

'Three of them came back,' said Mackenzie, 'didn't even make a mile. They said they got scared when they saw the cloud come down.'

'And what time was that?'

'According to Kelly, sometime around four o'clock, or thereabouts.'

'If they were so scared,' said West, 'why did they let Ella MacCall go up alone?'

'She was adamant, so they say. She didn't want to leave the island having seen nothing but the inside of a hotel room.'

'And they didn't try to stop her?'

'Holly Paterson says they did, but it was like talking to a brick wall.'

'So, who called rescue?'

'Megan Dalgleish,' said Mackenzie. 'She used the phone behind the bar and did the usual: 999.'

'Time?'

'8 pm, give or take.'

'Eight o'clock!' said Duncan. 'Why the hell did she leave it so late?'

'John McIver's words exactly. He was fizzing, and I can't say I blame him either.'

'Was there anything unusual about the body when they found it?'

'Not that I know of.'

'And did they find anything? Her phone, maybe?'

'What do you think?' said Mackenzie. 'Listen, no offence, but it was pitch black up there and they didn't have the chopper. If it wasn't for the wee doggie I doubt they'd have found her at all.'

'So, the question is,' said Duncan, 'why would a young lass be stupid enough to climb the mountain in summer clothes despite her pals warning her off?'

Mackenzie shrugged his shoulders and drained his mug.

'Who knows?' he said. 'Maybe it was a dare.'

West, apparently bored, disinterested, or preoccupied, rose to her feet and wandered slowly around the room, stopping to peruse a curious assortment of china knick-knacks sitting on the mantel shelf before checking her watch.

'What time do they stop serving?' she said.

Mackenzie glanced furtively at Duncan and smirked.

'Sorry?'

'Food. What time does the kitchen close?'

'Nine.'

'Good,' said West, as if talking to herself. 'The girls, how were they when they returned from Goat Fell? Their mood, were they happy? Sad? Worried? Upset?'

'No to all of the above,' said Mackenzie. 'Obviously I wasn't here but Kelly says they were their usual selves, relaxed as in not really fussed about anything. They had themselves some supper in the bar and then a few drinks.'

'How old are they?'

Mackenzie puffed his cheeks as he referred to his notes.

'Three are eighteen, that's including Ella MacCall, and Holly Paterson's the eldest at nineteen.'

'Isn't that a bit young for a girl to go yomping up a mountain unaccompanied?'

'Not really, miss. An experienced fifteen year old could do it.'

'But not an inexperienced eighteen year old, obviously. Was there anyone with them? A guide? A local who knows the path?'

'No-one,' said Mackenzie. 'I'll be frank, miss, no-one in their right mind would've headed up there, not anyone from these parts anyway.'

West, her green eyes glinting in the glow of the single overhead bulb, stared vacuously into space and paused.

'Next of kin,' she said. 'I assume you've already informed her family?'

'No,' said Mackenzie. 'She doesn't have any. According to Holly Paterson she was raised in care from the age of nine. Her parents died suddenly.'

'Suddenly?'

'RTC miss. A lorry rear-ended them on the motorway.'

'And I bet he got off with a couple of years,' said West as she grabbed her coat. 'The girls, did they arrive on foot?'

'They say they took a taxi from the terminal.'

'And have you checked that?'

'Sorry? I'm not with you.'

'Have you checked with the cab company? Have you found out who picked them up?'

'Well, no. I didn't think…'

'Do it now. We'll be upstairs.'

* * *

The twin room, tastefully furnished with two single wrought iron beds, a dresser, a wardrobe and an easy chair was – save for the glow of a flickering table lamp – as gloomy as the louring night sky. The girls, sitting side by side like subordinate siblings sulking under a curfew, jumped as Duncan, not waiting for an invitation, blundered into the room and hit the lights.

'Dear God, you look happy,' he said as a startled Holly Paterson shielded her eyes. 'I hope we've not kept you waiting.'

'No, you're alright,' said Holly. 'We've had Instagram to keep us busy.'

'In my day,' said West, smiling as she perched on the edge of the armchair, 'we had something called books. So, come on then, who's who?'

'I'm Holly, this is Kirsty, and that's Megan.'

'I'm Detective Inspector West and this is Detective Constable Reid.'

'Detective?' said Holly. 'How so? I mean, did Ella not just freeze to death?'

'It's a bit more complicated than that but it's nothing for you to worry about. So, how are you feeling?'

'Okay.'

'Just okay?'

'Aye. You know.'

'I do,' said West. 'It's never easy, losing a friend.'

'Well it's her own fault.'

'Is it? And why's that?'

'She was stupid. She should never have gone up there alone.'

'You're not wrong there,' said Duncan. 'Did you not try to stop her?'

'Aye, of course we did,' said Holly, 'but Ella's Ella. She's as stubborn as mule.'

West sat back, crossed her legs and smiled.

'She was single-minded then? The confident kind?'

'No. Anything but.'

'Really? Then why was she so determined to go it alone?'

Holly, her face devoid of emotion, stared at West and huffed a disgruntled sigh.

'You seem angry,' said West, intrigued by her ire, 'is that because of what's happened or, I don't know, something else maybe? Did she upset you? An argument, perhaps?'

'Not so much an argument,' said Holly. 'More a disagreement.'

'About going up the mountain?'

Holly glanced furtively at Kirsty and Megan, and lowered her head.

'Look, I know this can't be easy,' said West, 'but I've been through the mill myself so, come on, what was it?'

'If you must know, it was about this fella she's been seeing.'

'What about him?'

'We're not keen on him. He keeps turning up whenever we're out, it's like he's following us around, he's like some kind of stalker but Ella, she'll not have a word said against him.'

'So you've met him?'

'We have, aye.'

'And do you know his name?'

'Alessandro Ricci.'

'Sounds Italian.'

'He is,' said Holly. 'And he's old enough to be her father.'

'I see. And you're not happy about that?'

'It's pervy. He should be dating grannies.'

'Takes all sorts,' said West. 'So where did they meet?'

'Home. Irvine. That's all I know.'

'And what's so bad about him?'

'Everything.'

'Everything? Are you sure you're not just a teensy bit jealous?'

'Are you joking me?' said Holly, her lip curling with contempt. 'Absolutely not. We're just looking out for her, that's all. We didn't want to see her get hurt.'

'It's a bit late for that, hen,' said Duncan.

'See here, constable, he's nice enough on the outside. He's polite, a wee charmer, but he's a control freak. He tells her what to wear, what to eat, who she can see and who she can't. He's trouble, I'm telling you.'

'Is he married?'

'I've no idea.'

'So, let me guess,' said West, 'she had a cob on because she was here with you instead of being at home with him?'

'Aye. Maybe.'

'And you don't like the fact that he's coming between you and Ella. There's nothing wrong with that, it's perfectly understandable. I mean you've obviously known each other a long time.'

'We have,' said Holly, 'since school. We were all in the same class, well, except me. I was the year above.'

West stood, pulled her phone from her hip and, ignoring the missed call from Dougal, stared at her reflection in the window and tousled her already ruffled hair.

'Tell me, Holly,' she said. 'Why did you come to Arran?'

'No reason. We just like the boats. Any excuse to ride a ferry. This year we've done Bute, Cumbrae and Jura, and next month we're away to Lewis.'

'Good for you. Must cost a bit, though?'

'Don't be daft,' said Holly. 'It's cheaper than a night in a club and you don't have to put up with a bunch of neds off their heads on lager and laughing gas chasing you round the dance floor.'

'Do you sail at home then? Is this some kind of hobby of yours?'

'Do I look like I own a boat?'

'Actually,' said West, 'I was thinking more a sailing club.'

'Oh. Sorry. No.'

'Still, it can't be easy arranging time off together.'

'It's not that difficult,' said Holly. 'I'm the only one who works.'

'And what do you do?'

'McDonald's,' said Holly, clearly embarrassed. 'It's not great but it's a job, right? Ella, Megan and Kirsty, they're the clever ones. They've just started uni.'

'I see,' said West. 'And do they teach communication skills at this uni?'

Megan looked up from the myriad of photos posted under the hashtag *#instalove* and scowled at the interruption.

'I wouldn't know,' she said. 'Why?'

'Because you could do with some. You're not saying much.'

'Am I not? It must be the grief.'

'Yeah,' said West. 'That'll be it. So tell me, Megan, whose idea was it to go for a jaunt up Goat Fell?'

'Who do you think? Ella.'

'And she wanted you to go with her?'

'Aye.'

'So why didn't you?'

'Are you mad? Once that cloud came rolling in, that was us, gone.'

'So you had a little disagreement,' said West, 'and left her to it?'

'We did. It's not a crime, is it?'

'No, it's not. But why did you leave it so late to call the rescue services?'

'We were pissed off,' said Holly. 'We thought we'd let her stew a while. She was ruining the trip for all of us. We must have lost track of time.'

'Exactly,' said Megan. 'We lost track of time because we were actually enjoying ourselves.'

'And?'

'And what? When she didn't come back, I called 999.'

'Did she take anything with her on this wee expedition?' said Duncan. 'Food? Drink? A hat? Gloves? A whistle?'

'Aye, she did. A packet of cheese and onion, and a flask.'

'And have any of you done any hillwalking before?'

'Dream on,' said Megan. 'Even if we'd wanted to, frankly we're just not fit enough.'

'And is Ella?'

'I'd say so, aye. She plays netball and hockey.'

'Well that should've stood her in good stead,' said West, 'but there's one thing I don't get. If she didn't want to be here, why was she so adamant about climbing Goat Fell? If anything, I'd have thought she'd be heading for the next ferry home.'

'I've no idea,' said Megan. 'She just said it was something she had to do.'

'No,' said West. 'Everest was something Hillary had to do. The north face of the Eiger was something Bonington had to do. She's not in the same league, is she?'

West stood with her arms folded and stared at Kirsty who, having successfully avoided eye contact throughout the entire proceedings, had stayed mute.

'Kirsty,' she said. 'How was Ella just before you turned back?'

'The usual.'

'She didn't seem distant? Distracted? A bit tired maybe?'

'No,' said Kirsty. 'If anything, it's like she couldn't wait to get going.'

'And before you set off, from here I mean, did any of you have a drink to perk you up? A bit of Dutch courage?'

'No. Look, we like a wee bevvy, I'm not denying it, but not during the day. We're not jakeys.'

'Fair enough,' said West. 'Well I think we're almost done here. Two more questions and we'll be out of your hair. First off, whose room is this?'

'Me and Megan,' said Kirsty. 'Ella's next door with Holly.'

'And number two, how did you get here from the ferry?'

'Taxi,' said Megan.

'And do you remember the name of the cab company?'

'No.'

'The colour of the car?'

'No.'

'What about the driver? Do you remember what he looked like?'

'Scottish.'

'That's incredibly helpful,' said West as she turned for the door. 'Thanks for that. Okay, I may need to have a word with you in the morning so no sloping off before you've seen me, got that?'

'If you say so.'

'Good. Now, we're going to take a look at Ella's room. Holly, is that okay with you? Do you want to come with us?'

'No, you're alright. I think it's time we hit the bar.'

* * *

Ignoring the bed that appeared to have been occupied by someone with restless leg syndrome, Duncan turned his attention to a lilac rucksack atop the other whilst West, dropping to her hands and knees, searched underneath before standing and flipping the mattress.

'Anything?' she said.

'The usual,' said Duncan. 'Clothes, toiletries, and a purse. There's about thirty quid, some loose change, a provisional driving licence, and a bank card. That's it.'

Feeling about as confident as Columbo in a game of hunt the thimble, a deflated West sighed as she turned her attention to the empty wardrobe before rifling through the dresser when Duncan, sounding surprisingly buoyant, yelped with the kind of fervour normally reserved for Celtic scoring an away win.

'Get it up you!' he said, grinning as he held a pillow in one hand and a bright yellow Nokia in the other.

'Where was that?' said West.

'Pillowcase, miss. Looks like she was trying to hide it.'

'Nice one, Duncan. Check the log, see who she was last in touch with.'

'Someone called Al.'

'Alessandro,' said West. 'Has to be. Any texts? Voicemail?'

'Negative.'

'Right, we'll get Dougal to pull it apart when we get back. The question is, why didn't she have it with her? Why was she hiding it?'

'That's a hell of a question, miss, unless…'

'I'm listening.'

'…unless she had two.'

'Two phones? It's possible.'

'And she might have lost the other one on the mountain.'

'Right,' said West, 'nip down to the bar and ask the girls what number they have for Ella. Better still, say nothing about the phone, get them to call her. If that doesn't ring, then we'll know she's been up to something naughty.'

'Roger that, miss.'

'I'll be along in a minute. How are you feeling now?'

'How d'you mean?'

'Do you still feel like chucking up or shall we eat?'

* * *

Duncan folded his napkin, plopped it on the table and cursed the recurring bouts of queasiness brought about not by the mountain of macaroni cheese he'd forced down his neck but by the sight of West devouring a plateful of haggis nachos, the venison casserole, a side order of chips and a chocolate caramel tart.

'So,' said West, 'did you check Ella's number?'

'I did and it's not the Nokia. They all swear blind she's got a Samsung. A Galaxy something or other.'

'In that case let's assume that Ella MacCall was using the new phone to keep her relationship a secret from someone other than the girls.'

'Family?'

'Maybe.'

'So,' said Duncan waving the Nokia, 'will we give this Alessandro fella a wee call?'

'God no,' said West, 'we'll wait until Dougal's ripped it apart, which reminds me, I need to give him a bell.'

'Well, while you do that, I'll fetch us a couple of goldies.'

'You what?'

'Whisky, miss.'

'Nice one. Lochranza, please. And make it a double.'

* * *

West, one hand in her pocket, stood in the vestibule staring through the glass-fronted doors with the distant hum of the bar behind her and the sound of sleet lashing the treetops dead ahead.

'Dougal,' she said. 'Tell me you've gone home.'

'Not yet, miss. Something's up.'

'Anything juicy?'

'As a peach. Have you got a minute?'

'I certainly have but I've got a couple of things for you first. Number one, how's Jimbo? Been and gone I suppose.'

'Neither,' said Dougal. 'He never arrived.'

'What? Why? Has something happened?'

'No, no. He says a pal of his was worried about his daughter, she's gone AWOL apparently and he said he was going to try and track her down.'

'Typical Jimbo,' said West. 'I'll give him a bell later and see what the old sod's been up to. Right, next thing, I'm sending you the names and addresses of the girls involved with Ella MacCall. I want a background check on all three please, as quick as you can.'

'A background check? Are they not as innocent as they seem?'

'Far from it. They're being cagey about something and I need to know what and why.'

'No bother. Is everything else okay?'

'Yeah, all good, apart from Duncan.'

'How so?'

'Let's just say when it comes to sailing, he's no Captain Birds Eye. So, what did you want to talk about?'

'That fella on Sandgate, miss. The one who walked into a machete.'

'What about him? Is he okay?'

'Oh aye,' said Dougal. 'It's a wee scratch. To be fair, I could've done more damage with a butter knife. Anyways, it turns out this fella's a journalist by the name of Nick Riley.'

'And being a journo, he's rubbed someone up the wrong way?'

'In one, miss. I'll not bore you with the details just now but basically he wrote an article on how easy it is for folk in the EU with a criminal record to hop on a plane and get themselves over here.'

'It's not just the EU, Dougal, it's the whole bleedin' world.'

'Right enough. Anyway, he came across this fella from Siena in Italy who's been here for two years.'

'And?'

'And he's got form,' said Dougal. 'He did six months for harassing, threatening and persecuting behaviour…'

'You mean stalking?'

'Aye, but that's not all. He was also charged with three counts of manslaughter but released due to insufficient evidence. One week later he pitched up here, in Ayrshire.'

'And this Riley bloke,' said West, 'he reckons he's the one who boshed him with the machete?'

'Exactly. It's a fella by the name of Ricci. Alessandro Ricci.'

* * *

Content to bide his time savouring the spicy aroma of his single malt, Duncan sat staring wistfully into space opposite an agitated Mackenzie who, keen to clock off, breathed a sigh of relief as West blustered through the bar, snatched the tumbler from the table, and downed her whisky in one.

'Are you okay?' said Duncan. 'You look like you've seen a ghost.'

'Well there's something spooky going on, that's for sure. I need a refill, do the honours would you?'

'Are you sure?'

'I'm positive,' said West. 'You won't believe what I've just heard. Constable Mackenzie, have you knocked off yet?'

'Not quite, miss. I've another half an hour yet.'

'Too bad. You've just missed out on a free drink. So, what's up?'

'I just dropped by to tell you that the cab company's dragging their heels. They'll get back to me as soon as they've quietened down but it may a take wee while.'

'Well, I haven't got time to wait around for them,' said West. 'Get on to CalMac, I want a full passenger list for the ferry the girls were on and any CCTV they've got of the terminal portside. It's the passengers disembarking I'm interested in and I also want a list of all the vehicles on the same crossing, got that?'

'Miss.'

'Oh, and before I forget, give Duncan the address for this McIver bloke. I'll be at the bar.'

Chapter 6

Alone in the confines of the custody suite, Munro, hands clasped behind his back, stared solemnly at the bank of blue, steel doors and drew a short, sharp breath as his thoughts turned to his erstwhile colleague and friend Alexander Craig and the untimely death of his young daughter, Agnes, who was brutally slain by a sadistic psychopath as she lay sleeping in her bed. He thanked God that Sophie had not succumbed to a similar fate.

Still smarting from the psychological effects of leading an investigation so close to home, he cursed under his breath and spun on his heels as the door behind him creaked open.

'Well?' he said, his icy blue eyes glinting in the harsh overhead light. 'How is she?'

'Not great but she's well enough to travel.'

'Are there any signs of… you know, *interference*?'

'I can't say,' said the doctor with a sympathetic shake of the head. 'We'd have to give her a full examination to find that out but on the positive side there's no sign of any bruising.'

'Your optimism astounds me. And on the negative?'

'Well, she's clearly not intoxicated but she's definitely taken something.'

'Explain yourself man!'

'She's weak,' said the doctor. 'Physically weak. Of course that could be from of a lack of sustenance but her reactions are slower than I'd expect, her blood pressure's a wee bit low, and she's not been to the bathroom since she was brought in.'

'Good grief!' said Munro. 'I'm not after a prognosis! What exactly does that mean?'

'It means, and remember I can't be certain about this, it looks as though she's taken a sedative of sorts.'

'As I thought. So, we need bloods.'

'Aye, we do indeed.'

'How long?' said Munro. 'For the results I mean. It's urgent.'

'I'll send the sample by courier now but it's normally a couple of days before…'

'No, no, no! Did you not hear me? I said it's urgent!'

The doctor, already miffed at missing his supper, checked his watch and, about to absolve himself of any responsibility when it came to sending samples for analysis, thought the better of it as his hapless gaze was met with Munro's intimidating stare.

'Okay,' he said. 'I'll nip across to the hospital at Crosshouse, it's only a couple of miles away. I'll wait while they run some tests. Give me an hour or two.'

'You've an hour,' said Munro. 'One hour. And you're to call me as soon as you're done. Do I make myself clear?'

'Perfectly. Oh, one more thing, the lassie has a wee tattoo on the small of her back. It's not a professional number, it looks homemade.'

'By jiminy, you're trying my patience, you balloon! How in God's name could she tattoo herself on the back?'

'I really have no idea, Inspector. Mister. Whatever it is you call yourself, but I suggest she gets it checked out.

Could turn nasty if she's got an infection. Perhaps you'd care to have a word. Cheery-bye.'

* * *

Unlike a sommelier whose discerning sense of smell could differentiate between the subtle notes of a sublime chardonnay and the delicate fragrance of a smooth sauvignon, Munro's uneducated palate was limited to detecting the difference between rump and sirloin which, as a consequence, resulted in a reaction bordering on anaphylactic shock when he once mistook a habanero for a cherry tomato. Alarmed by the palpitations pounding in his chest, he pulled a neatly pressed handkerchief from his breast pocket and dabbed his forehead, his deep breathing interrupted by the unexpected arrival of Sergeant Ryan.

'Mr Munro,' he said. 'Are you okay?'

'Aye, never better. What's up?'

'A wee favour.'

'I've no time for favours, laddie,' said Munro. 'I'm about to run Miss Jackson home.'

'No, no. You misunderstand. It's me doing you the favour.'

'How so?'

Ryan proffered his hand and slipped Munro a folded sheet of paper.

'It's an address,' he said. 'You should go there now.'

'Stop havering and explain yourself!'

'Just go. I'm sure she'll not mind waiting another half an hour.'

* * *

From the first daffodils of spring to the umber days of autumn, the sprawling Kay Park – with its vast lake and abundance of wildlife – was enjoyed from dawn until dusk by love-struck teens, parents with buggies, kids on bicycles, and dog walkers exercising their tireless hounds but, after dark in the depths of winter, the thirty-acre site adopted a less welcoming atmosphere.

Drawn by the array of flashing blue lights, Munro, hands in pockets with his cap pulled low over his brow, marched through the persistent sleet towards a row of leafless trees, their silhouetted limbs twisted and gnarled like tortured victims of a forest fire.

A doleful-looking officer with a face like a wet weekend squinted at Munro and, recognising the Sillitoe tartan around his cap, raised the cordon and beckoned him through.

'DS McCrae?' he said, wiping his nose with the back of his hand.

'No.'

'Oh. I just assumed… I mean, I was told he was on his way.'

'Well you'll not miss him,' said Munro. 'He rides a scooter that sounds like a wasp trapped in a can of fizzy pop. In the meantime, you'll have to settle for me. The name's Munro.'

'Of course it is,' said the constable. 'Sergeant Ryan said you were coming. Sorry but we've not had time to get a marquee up yet.'

'That's why God gave us umbrellas. So, what's the story?'

'A young girl, sir. A fella with a Lab spotted her not even an hour ago.'

'Any ideas?'

'Not really,' said the constable, shrugging his shoulders. 'She still has her purse and her phone so it's not a mugging, which means she was probably attacked, attempted rape maybe. One thing's for sure, she's not having a wee lie down for the hell of it.'

'If you fancy a career as a comedian, sonny, I can arrange for you to give up your day job.'

'Sorry, no offence, I was just…'

'Have you made an ID?'

'Not formally, sir, no. But if the purse belongs to her then her name's Sullivan. Miss Jessica Sullivan.'

Munro threw his head back, closed his eyes and drew a long, deep breath.

'Dear God,' he said, gritting his teeth.

'Sorry, I didn't catch that.'

'Déjà vu, laddie. Déjà vu. Next of kin?'

'The lads are at the house now but there's nobody home.'

Recognising at once the ripped jeans and denim jacket as described by Mrs Sullivan, Munro pushed his cap to the back of his head, approached the familiar figure hunched over the body and crouched down beside him, his eyes narrowing as the beam from his penlight bounced off her rosy cheeks.

'Mr McLeod,' he said. 'You've obviously not got a home to go to either.'

'Mr Munro. I thought you were retired.'

'Dinnae be fooled, my presence is nothing less than serendipitous. Although I have to say, I do appear to be tied to this blessed job with a bungee rope. How long?'

'A couple of hours, tops.'

'And what do you think?'

'Well, I'm not ruling out a cardiac arrest,' said McLeod, 'it's more common than you think amongst the younger generation, especially when you consider the concoctions they're so fond of drinking.'

'Aye, right enough,' said Munro. 'In my day it was pale ale or lager, and if you couldnae afford that, it was down to the hardware store for a bottle of methylated spirit.'

'Oh aye. I'm sure it was.'

'Now, unless you're about to tell me otherwise,' said Munro as he scrutinized the body, 'then I'm of the opinion that this lassie wasnae attacked. There's no sign of a struggle, not even a hair out of place.'

McLeod pulled the mask from his face, ran his fingers through his bushy, red beard, and turned to face Munro.

'My thoughts exactly,' he said. 'This lassie wasn't dragged to the ground or pushed like she'd been ambushed. If she had, she'd have her arms out like she was trying to save herself. No, no. She fell alright, or more to the point, collapsed on the spot. She's a nasty wee graze to the side of her head where she hit the deck.'

'So?'

McLeod stared pensively at Jessica's face and paused before speaking.

'I can't say for certain, not yet, not until I've run a few tests but if it's not her heart then, going by her bloodshot eyes, I'd hazard a guess at...'

'Benzodiazepine.'

'Top of the class, Mr Munro. What makes you say that?'

'Instinct.'

'And?'

'And the fact that she may not be the first.'

'How so?'

'You'll find out soon enough,' said Munro. 'See here, Mr McLeod, correct me if I'm wrong but this Benzodiazepine, it doesnae hang around, does it? Once it's taken?'

'It does not. Ten minutes on average, maybe sooner if it was a strong dose, by which I mean a fatal one.'

Munro glanced over his shoulder gauging the distance to the entrance on the street.

'Then there's every chance she wasnae alone when she entered the park. Either that or she took the Benzo' just before cutting through here. Let me know for sure just as soon as possible, would you? You have my number.'

'I will indeed,' said McLeod. 'By the way, I'm curious, how come Charlie's not dealing with this?'

'Charlie? The object of your unrequited love?'

'Very good. Let's just say we appear to have a mutual fear of commitment.'

'Then you're in luck,' said Munro as he stood. 'She's in Arran.'

'Holidays?'

'Aye. A busman's. What's the matter, Mr McLeod? You've a look of trouble about you.'

'You say she's in Arran?'

'Correct.'

'And is she there for the lassie on Goat Fell?'

'I assume so. I'm afraid I'm not up to speed on the whys and wherefores concerning her trip. Why?'

'Because the girl on the mountain, name of MacCall, she'd taken roofies.'

'Roofies?'

'Rohypnol. And when I say taken, I mean somebody probably slipped it into her drink.'

Munro stared at McLeod, his face riddled with angst.

'Exactly how many cases involving Rohypnol have you dealt with?'

'Throughout my career? MacCall makes two.'

'That's two more than me,' said Munro, cocking his head as the drone of a scooter drew near. 'Mr McLeod, correct me if I'm wrong but I thought Rohypnol was a banned substance?'

'Yes and no,' said McLeod. 'Yes, generally speaking, but it's available under private prescription.'

'From a GP?'

'From any GP.'

'Right, that's me away. Young Dougal will attend to you now.'

* * *

Intent on maintaining his image as an ice-cool member of the Genoese *scooteristi,* Dougal resisted the temptation to bulk-up his slight physique with overweight leathers like an extra from Mad Max III, choosing instead to protect his wiry frame from the elements with nothing more than a fluorescent Canali blouson and a thick, woollen scarf.

Looking as happy as a dog with two tails, he hopped off the scooter, lifted his goggles, and greeted Munro with a maniacal grin.

'Boss!' he said. 'I wasn't expecting to see you!'

'Life is full of surprises, Dougal.'

'Did you happen to find your friend's… jeez-oh, that's not her, is it?'

'No, no. Fortunately, it is not.'

'Oh, that is a relief.'

'Were you not in your bed when they called you out?'

'No, no,' said Dougal. 'I was looking into the mysterious case of the man with the machete. It's a belter.'

'And have you found him?'

'I have a suspect, I'll have a wee word tomorrow. What brings you here anyway?'

'The fickle hand of fate,' said Munro, 'and if I'm not mistaken, it belongs to the Reaper. I'll leave you to it, laddie, I have to run Miss Jackson back to Carsethorn just now, but I'll see you tomorrow.'

'Right you are, boss. Incidentally, I had a look at those ticketing websites for you and…'

'I appreciate your efforts,' said Munro, 'but it's not important anymore, they didnae go to the concert. It was all a front, a ruse to hide some night time shenanigans.'

'Shenanigans? Were they up to no good?'

'See for yourself,' said Munro as he nodded towards the body and pulled his phone from his pocket. 'I have to take this. Doctor?'

'Mr Munro. I'm still waiting for more results but I thought I'd call you with the good news.'

'The word "good" is debateable.'

'We can't say for certain whether Miss Jackson was given Flunitrazepam or not, not without doing more detailed tests.'

'Well she was given something man!' said Munro. 'Enough to knock her out!'

'Aye, I'm not denying that,' said doctor, 'but all I can say at this stage is that it could've been anything from a Benzo' to painkillers. Sorry, but that's the nub of it.'

Chapter 7

Despite a steaming-hot shower in a spume of citrus-scented body wash, copious amounts of deodorant, and a generous splash of eau de toilette, an unshaven Duncan Reid – dressed in a manky pair of jeans, brown biker boots and a battered leather jacket, with a hairstyle loosely based on a squirrel's drey – still managed to look like he'd spent the night roughing it amongst the flora and fauna of the neighbouring woods with only a munchy box and a bottle of barley wine for company.

Thinking he'd impress his superior by finishing breakfast before she'd even risen from her bed, he made his way downstairs to the dining room only to be confronted by a serene-looking West casually sipping coffee as she waded through a wodge of A4 papers.

'Alright mate,' she said. 'You having a lie-in?'

'No, miss,' said Duncan, spying the empty plate. 'Have you already eaten?'

'Yup. Smoked kippers, scrambled eggs, bacon, oh, and a couple of sausages. Blooming great it was too. You'd best order something quick if you're hungry.'

'Oh, there's no rush. It's just the back of seven and they serve breakfast until ten.'

'Yeah, but we're off in twenty so you'd best get a wiggle on or you'll have to make do with a lovely bowl of granola.'

Panicked by the thought of surviving the next five hours on a bowl of cereal designed for sheep and badgers, Duncan hastily ordered a traditional fry-up and returned to the table.

'Anything interesting?' he said, nodding towards the papers as he helped himself to coffee.

'I'm not sure yet. It's the passenger list and vehicle inventory from CalMac.'

'Really? Is Mackenzie here then?'

'Nah, it was waiting for me in reception,' said West as she plucked her phone from her hip. 'He must've dropped it off late last night. Speak of the devil. Constable Mackenzie, you're up bright and early. How's tricks?'

'Aye, all good, miss. Yourself?'

'Tickety-boo.'

'Are you up for a wee chat?'

'Yup. DC Reid's with me so I'll stick you on speaker.'

'Okay,' said Mackenzie. 'Excluding private hire, as you know there's really only two taxi firms that operate from the ferry terminal and neither says they had a fare with four girls off the 6:55.'

'That's odd,' said Duncan. 'They're adamant they didn't walk here, so why would they lie about getting a taxi?'

'You know your trouble, don't you?' said West with a smirk. 'You're too suspicious.'

'I thought that was part and parcel of the job.'

'Relax. They probably cadged a lift off some poor unsuspecting tourist.'

'Aye, I think you might be right,' said Mackenzie. 'I took the liberty of looking at the CCTV footage from the quayside…'

'You are keen,' said West. 'I like that.'

'I've sent you the same but I've got the girls, clear as day, waiting for a car to roll off the ferry, then they all hop in.'

'Excellent. Have you got a make on it?'

'I have indeed,' said Mackenzie. 'It's a Vauxhall. Will I give you the index?'

'Yeah, go on,' said West as she shuffled through the papers.

'It's sierra alpha, one six, oscar charlie golf.'

West ran a finger down the list of vehicles, turned the page and paused, a look of consternation on her face.

'That car,' she said, 'SA16 OCG. It was on the return leg too.'

'But that doesn't make any sense,' said Duncan. 'Who in their right mind would take a ferry from the mainland only to go back thirty minutes later?'

'My guess is they either realised they'd left the gas on and legged it back before the house blew up or they made the trip for no other reason than to drop the girls off.'

'Like a taxi from Kilmarnock?' said Mackenzie.

'Possibly, although I reckon that's a bit too extravagant considering their budget.'

'Either way, something doesn't add up,' said Duncan as he left the room. 'I think it's time I had a word with them. I'll not be long.'

'Find out if there's any cameras here while you're at it,' said West, 'front entrance and reception.'

'Roger that.'

'Constable Mackenzie, are you still there?'

'Miss.'

'Do me favour,' said West. 'Find out if that vehicle booked a return ticket in advance or if it just showed up, would you?'

'No bother.'

'Now, what about the driver? Is the footage clear enough to get a gander at his face?'

'No chance. It's dark and there's too many reflections, not to mention the sleet.'

West pondered the situation as she drained the last dregs of coffee from her cup.

'CalMac,' she said. 'Have they got cameras on board the ferries? On the car decks?'

'I'm ahead of you, miss,' said Mackenzie. 'Leave it with me and I'll call you back.'

'Nice one. Quick as you can please, we have to head home this afternoon.'

West, amused by the fact that as a young DC her presence on the force was regarded as nothing more than a token nod to the equal opportunities commission but as a DI, male members of the same fraternity made it their mission to impress her with uncharacteristic displays of diligence, thanked Mackenzie for his sterling work and terminated the call.

She smiled as a burly chef with his sleeves rolled to the elbow arrived at the table bearing an oval platter laden with enough food to feed a family of four and swiped the only slice of toast from the plate, dusting crumbs from her lips as an irate Duncan returned from reception.

'You'll not believe it, miss,' he said, grabbing a knife and fork. 'The girls, they've checked out already.'

'You what?' said West. 'Cheeky blighters. I told them to stay put until my say-so.'

'I just spoke with the landlady, that Kelly Baxter woman, she says they went for the eight o'clock.'

'Oh well, look on the bright side, it gives us more time with McIver.'

'You don't seem that bothered. If it was me, I'd be raging.'

'What's the point?' said West. 'We know where they live, we'll catch up with them later. Cameras?'

'Negative, miss. Baxter says she prides herself on running *a trouble-free establishment*, she says they're not necessary.'

'Nice to know there's still some places you can go without being spied on, I suppose. Now, eat your breakfast before it gets cold.'

Duncan glanced at his plate and then at West.

'What's up?' she said.

'Toast,' said Duncan. 'Someone's stolen my toast.'

'In a place like this? Unheard of. I'd call the cops if I were you. I'll be outside on the blower to Dougal.'

* * *

With her shoulders twitching against the crisp, morning breeze, West – shielding her eyes from the low-lying sun – filled her lungs with the damp, musty smell of the woods and called Dougal who, despite a sleepless night in front of his computers, sustained by a couple of litres of Irn-Bru and a family-sized packet of chocolate chip cookies, sounded as chirpy as ever.

'Miss! Am I glad to hear from you!'

'Nice to know I'm missed,' said West. 'Listen, I need you to do something for me, a vehicle check please.'

'Can I interrupt?' said Dougal as the words tumbled from his mouth. 'Sorry but there's something you need to know, I've been doing those background checks you asked for and you'll not believe what I've…'

'Dougal!'

'Aye?'

'Shut up! Now, take a deep breath and count to ten.'

'One, nine, ten.'

'God give me strength. Okay, start again. Slowly.'

'Sorry, miss, I've not slept. It must be the sugar.'

'As long as that's all it is.'

'The girls,' said Dougal. 'Megan Dalgleish, Holly Paterson, and Kirsty Young. They're all clean.'

'Well, that's good.'

'Aye. And like most young folk, they're not shy about letting the world know what they've been up to.'

'I don't follow.'

'Social media,' said Dougal. 'Places they've been, clothes they've bought, food they've eaten. Facebook, Twitter, Snapchat, you name it, they're on it.'

'So, nothing out of the ordinary then?' said West. 'Nothing that could help us out?'

'Not with them, no. But see here, I've also been looking at Ella MacCall and there's something not quite right.'

'Go on.'

'She's not like the others. She's not mad on social media but she does have a Facebook page. There's a bunch of grainy photos up there and a handful of videos. She looks like one of those arty types, you know, an amateur film-maker.'

'So, what's the big deal?' said West.

'She's the subject of the films.'

'Oh, is that all?' said West. 'Well maybe she's not a film-maker after all, maybe she wants to be an actress.'

'No, no,' said Dougal. 'The thing is, miss, this isn't acting, it's for real and it looks like she had some sort of a death wish.'

'You're probably over-reacting,' said West. 'The mind plays tricks when you've not had enough sleep.'

'No disrespect, miss, but that's not it. See here, there's a film of her in Glasgow on Byres Road, standing on the kerb during the rush hour. She's completely motionless, then just as a bus comes hurtling down the street, she steps out. Right in front of it.'

'What? Was she hurt?'

'No. The driver braked just in time but there's probably a few claims for whiplash from the passengers.'

'And you're sure it's her?'

'Positive. I even ran it by Doctor McLeod and he recognised her straight away. Listen, there's another film, a similar thing, only this time it's at the harbour in Troon.'

'She gets about a bit, doesn't she?'

'She's standing right on the edge of the dock outside the fish market so there's plenty of folk milling about, then she closes her eyes, leans forward and just topples in. Head first.'

'Well, she was pretty sporty and fit. I'm assuming she could swim.'

'If she could,' said Dougal, 'she didn't feel like it. She bobbed about on the surface until some fella off a trawler moored nearby jumped in and rescued her. If it wasn't for him, she'd have gone under, that's for sure.'

'Well, if you're right, then what the hell was she playing at? Trying to top herself?'

'I'm not quite sure but I'm thinking her trip up Goat Fell may not have been an accident after all.'

'Hold on,' said West. 'If she was on a suicide mission, then who the hell was filming her?'

'That's the question. I'll try and get in the back-end this afternoon, see if I can find where they came from. Oh, and there's something else.'

'There always is with you.'

'Every photo and every film has been liked by one fella in particular. Somebody calling themselves Alex Ricci.'

'Ricci?'

'Aye,' said Dougal. 'It's possible he's just one of her followers but I'm wondering if this Alex fella is actually Alessandro. Alessandro Ricci. The same Alessandro Ricci who had a wee pop at the journalist.'

'It has to be,' said West. 'Apart from the fact you don't get that many Riccis to the pound, I'll let you into a little secret. Ella MacCall was having a fling with him.'

'Are you joking me?'

'I kid you not. So, what's your plan?'

'Well, I'm away to question him about the attack on the journalist later, I thought I'd see how he reacts if I drop Ella MacCall into the conversation.'

'Okay good,' said West. 'But no heroics, got that? Don't take any risks. If it was him then he might be a bit unhinged.'

'No danger of that, miss,' said Dougal. 'I'm taking back up.'

'Well ring me as soon as you're done and if he kicks off do him on suspicion of GBH. I need to have a word with him about MacCall anyway. Now, before you go, that vehicle check please.'

'No bother. Fire away and I'll do it now.'

'Sierra alpha, one six, oscar charlie golf.'

With his fingers flying across the keyboard like a pianist on a week's worth of crack, Dougal ran a search with the DVLA on one computer whilst simultaneously running a trace through the PNC on the other.

'Okay,' he said, his eyes flashing between the screens. 'It's a Vauxhall Insignia. Silver. Two litre diesel turbo. It's taxed and the MOT's not due until September. The registered keeper's a Miss Helen Sullivan of Woodstock Street, Kilmarnock.'

'Good. Now I know it's a lot to ask but once you've collared this Ricci bloke maybe you could…'

'Jeez-oh!' said Dougal. 'Just a minute miss. There's already been a call out on it.'

'What? How come? Impossible.'

'Give me a second. Oh, they've found it.'

'Blimey, that was quick.'

'It was involved in an incident in Kilmarnock, an abduction by the looks of it and…'

West, perturbed by the sudden silence as Dougal's words tailed off, checked the signal on her phone and waved it frantically in the air in the hope of being reconnected.

'Dougal!' she said. 'What's up? Are you there?'

'Aye, miss,' said Dougal, sounding slightly dazed. 'Sorry, I've just thought of something. I was on a call last night, a wee lassie found in a park. When I got there, so was the boss.'

'Jimbo?'

'Aye.'

'Crap. I don't like the sound of this.'

'Remember he was trying to find a girl who'd gone missing? His pal's daughter?'

'Yeah. Oh God, that wasn't her was it?'

'No. But I'm sorry to say it was her friend.'

'Okay,' said West. 'Don't think me callous, Dougal, but how is this relevant?'

'This friend of hers, her name was Sullivan and she was last seen outside Bakers nightclub getting into a silver Insignia. It's the same one.'

Chapter 8

Leaving a grateful, if not relieved, Paul Jackson under strict instructions to treat his daughter with the sympathy she deserved as an innocent victim of circumstance rather than berate her for staying out late, a fatigued and somewhat morose Munro – fearing that his palpitations were a sign of something serious and not, as a man of simple tastes, the after-effects of overdosing on elephant garlic and Red Bull – reluctantly abandoned his journey home in favour of a trip to the accident and emergency department. After being rushed through to ambulatory care, any praise he'd harboured for the cardiology consultant's assiduous approach to his condition dissipated when he deemed his apparent arrhythmia to be symptomatic of an unhealthy lifestyle rather than the consequence of a stressful occupation.

As someone who considered himself to be in fine fettle he agreed, albeit begrudgingly, to a series of thorough, though mercifully non-invasive checks, and duly suffered the indignity of an ECG, a stress test, an echocardiogram, and a chest X-ray before parting company with six vials worth of blood and leaving three hours later with the news that his arteries were as clogged as the M8 on a bank holiday weekend and the supercilious advice that unless he rest-up and change his diet he would shoot to the top of the list for a triple by-pass or, if he preferred to avoid the inconvenience of an operation, a shady spot alongside his wife in the local cemetery.

Advising the staff in a terse but polite manner that his BP, at 139 over 80, was probably the result of his aversion to hospital environments exacerbated by the fact that he'd not eaten for almost twenty-four hours, he left the hospital pining for something more substantial than the out-of-date bar of Kendall Mint Cake in the glove box, and sped along a deserted A76 towards Ayr with the dulcet tones of Radio Four and the rumble of his belly for company.

Driven by desperation and the fact that not even the greasiest of greasy spoons was open for business at 6:00 am, he was forced, against his better judgement, to stop at a branch of an inexplicably popular chain of coffee shops for a pot of tea, an over-priced bacon roll, and a bowl of porridge which, given its cloying consistency and stark resemblance to wallpaper paste, could have been used to successfully hang two rolls of woodchip or decoupage an entire wardrobe.

Wincing at the insipid taste of his watery brew, he set the cup to one side, popped a couple of aspirin with a glass of tepid tap water and checked his phone, cursing at the missed call from McLeod and the subsequent voicemail informing him that Jessica Sullivan had tested positive for abnormally high levels of codeine phosphate.

* * *

Having supplemented his sugar intake with a double dose of caffeine and a stale chocolate doughnut, Dougal – looking as if he'd just prised his tongue from the terminal of a twelve-volt battery – sat wide-eyed, reviewing a draft copy of the article written by Nick Riley in preparation for his unscheduled meeting with Alessandro Ricci.

'*...with his handmade loafers and cashmere sweaters, a healthy bank balance and a hillside villa in his native Tuscany, the sixty-one-year-old Alessandro Ricci looks every inch the successful businessman he purports to be.*

So why would the suave, silver-haired, bon viveur choose to give up the Siena sunshine for a life in Ayrshire? Was it the lure of the local Italian community? A fondness for our rugged landscape? Or was it perhaps that he'd developed a taste for neeps and tatties?

The answer is no to all of the above. Signor Ricci arrived on these shores in a bid to escape the hostility of his friends and associates, and the wrath of the law.

Released after a five-month sentence for assault and what is now recognised as "stalking", he returned home in an audacious bid to rebuild his life under the watchful gaze of his neighbours. However, whilst some regarded his guilt as questionable, the majority of locals in this traditionally Catholic and family-orientated society found his presence intolerable.

His victim, a seventeen-year-old college student who, having been raised by a single parent, looked upon him as a father figure, admitted falling for his debonair charm but ended the relationship when his coercive behaviour turned to physical abuse. Fearing for her safety, she ignored his threats of reprisals and reported him to the police.

The irrefutable evidence which resulted in Ricci's conviction was based on video footage, text messages and conversations the girl had had the temerity to record on her mobile phone.

After sentencing, many of Ricci's supporters, coincidentally those with a vested interest in his business empire, described the allegations as spurious and the outcome of the trial a travesty of justice, statements they retracted six months later when Ricci fell under the spotlight again.

Claiming to have been woken between the hours of 1 and 2 a.m. by the desperate cries of his female companion, Ricci, in a sworn statement, declared he'd ventured outside only to find her lying face down in the swimming pool, going on to describe her demise as "an unfortunate incident" and blaming the accident on muscle cramps and the girl's obvious inability to handle her drink.

The post-mortem, however, told a different story. An analysis of body fluids revealed only a token amount of alcohol in her system, in fact, the equivalent of less than half a glass. It also revealed a high amount of what the coroner described as a psychoactive drug.

Ricci was arrested, questioned and bailed whilst the investigation continued, during which time two similar cases occurred. Both were within a one-mile radius of Ricci's home. Both were single girls under the age of twenty. And both were victims of a sexual assault.

Ricci was re-arrested and charged with three counts of murder when a second search of his premises uncovered a substantial supply of the drug Temazepam which, though no evidence of such existed on his medical records, he claimed was used to treat his insomnia.

For readers unfamiliar with Temazepam, traces of which were found in all three of Ricci's alleged victims, it is a member of the class of drugs known as Benzodiazepines and is similar to Rohypnol, more commonly known as "the date-rape drug."

In a bizarre twist of fate, the judge presiding over Ricci's trial dismissed the evidence as circumstantial before pleading with the prosecution to return with conclusive proof that he was without doubt the perpetrator. Ricci was duly released and, according to his neighbours, vanished some days later.

At liberty to roam across Europe, a privilege afforded him under EU law, he slipped unnoticed into this country four months ago, assuming the identity of an entrepreneur looking for a new business venture.

Should any of his friends, former colleagues, or the Italian authorities be at all concerned for his welfare, I can assure them that he is in rude wealth and, for the time being at least, leading an understandably quiet life here in western Scotland.

According to unofficial figures it is worth remembering that Ricci is just one of a substantial number of criminals who have arrived in the UK after fleeing their homeland whilst on bail or under caution…'

Given the early hour and his heightened state of awareness, Dougal, already on tenterhooks, leapt at the unexpected sound of footsteps thumping along the corridor.

'Sorry to disappoint you,' said a sullen-faced Munro as he blew through the door, 'but I've not brought breakfast and it's not for want of trying either.'

'No bother,' said Dougal, his cheeks billowing with relief. 'I'm too wired to eat. Are you okay?'

'If I'm honest, no.'

'What's up?'

'Food poisoning. I think.'

'Oh dear, is it serious?'

'Knowing my luck,' said Munro, 'it's probably listeria so I'll be out of your way soon enough.'

'I think you need a decent brew.'

'Aye, that would be most welcome. Listen, Dougal, have you heard from Charlie recently?'

'I have. They're back this afternoon.'

'And did she mention anything about the lassie on Goat Fell?'

'Nothing new,' said Dougal. 'I ran a check on the girls who were with her but nothing so far. Why? Is something bothering you?'

'Aye. Did McLeod not say she was drugged?'

'He did. Is that not a bit unusual?'

'Around here,' said Munro, 'once is unusual. Twice is disconcerting. Three times gives me the heebie-jeebies.'

'Three? But there's only Ella MacCall and Jessica Sullivan.'

'And Sophie Jackson.'

'Jeez-oh, your pal's daughter? I didn't know. How is she?'

'Aye, she's okay,' said Munro sipping his tea, 'but I have to admit, if I was still employed in an official capacity, I'd kill for another wee word with that Sullivan woman about her daughter. Dinnae get me wrong, I've every sympathy for her tragic loss but the fact remains that it was

Jessica who led Sophie astray and it's only by the grace of God that you're not having to deal with another murder.'

'Right enough,' said Dougal, 'but if it was me then it's the fella who dosed her up I'd be wanting a word with.'

'Well that's not happening until you've done your homework.'

'As it happens, I'm revising right now.'

'Oh aye? What's the story?'

'Once upon a time there was a man with a machete...'

Munro rolled his eyes and pulled up a chair.

'Okay, I'm hooked,' he said. 'Go on.'

'...only this man is not who he seems. He's got form for stalking.'

'Is that so?'

'And he was charged with three counts of murder involving Temazepam.'

'By jiminy! Then why have I not heard of him?'

'Cos he's Italian, boss,' said Dougal. 'Name of Alessandro Ricci. He used to live in Siena but now he's here. On business, apparently.'

'Dear God. Let's hope it's not another coffee shop.'

'Somehow I don't think that's on the cards. The fella he attacked is a journalist, he's dropping by later with some more info he thinks we might find useful.'

'And this Ricci fellow, have you interviewed him yet?'

'I'm on my way now. Have you got your car with you?'

'What do you think?'

'Would you like to give me a lift?'

'And why would I want to do that?'

'Because,' said Dougal grinning like a fool, 'the vehicle used to abduct Jessica Sullivan belongs to one Helen Sullivan.'

'Her mother?'

'Aye, and not only that, it was on the ferry to Arran, the same ferry as Ella MacCall.'

'Jumping Jehoshaphat! Have you located it?'

'We have, boss. It's in the yard, SOCOs are going over it as we speak.'

'Well, that's good news, laddie, but tell me, what on earth has this to do with the Italian gentleman?'

'He shares the same address as Helen Sullivan.'

* * *

Apart from a single harried commuter scurrying to work with his coat buttoned against the cold and a couple of lackadaisical kids more interested in their phones than arriving at school on time, Woodstock Street, unlike the rest of the town centre, was eerily quiet.

Munro, with two uniformed officers tailing his Peugeot in a patrol car, stopped outside Sullivan's house and smirked as a shadowy figure appeared behind the curtains in an upstairs window.

'Someone's expecting us,' he said. 'I do hope they've got the kettle on.'

Dougal unclipped his safety belt and opened the door.

'I'll just tell the lads to sit tight unless we need them.'

'No, no,' said Munro pointing out the path that led to the rear of the house. 'Tell your pals to get themselves round the back. Watching a middle-aged woman trying to vault a garden fence is not a pretty sight, I can tell you.'

Devoid of make-up and clearly in no hurry to greet the outside world, a dishevelled Helen Sullivan, wrapped in a dressing gown with an unlit cigarette clasped between her lips, opened the door and shivered against the biting breeze.

'Oh, it's yourself,' she said. 'Did you find her? Young Sophie?'

'We did,' said Munro. 'It's kind of you to ask. And we also found Jessica. You have my condolences.'

'Accidents happen,' said Sullivan. 'She's not a wean. She knew what she was getting herself into.'

'How so?'

'The crowd she hung out with. It was only a matter of time. If you lay down with dogs, Mr Munro, you get fleas.'

'I cannae argue with that but forgive me, this is your daughter we're talking about.'

'Don't lecture me on parenting,' said Sullivan, 'we didn't get on, okay? Never have.'

'You'll not mind me asking if you've seen her then?'

'You mean have I identified the body? Aye. It's her alright. So, what is it you're after?'

'Just a few questions.'

Sullivan cast a sideways at Dougal and flicked her head.

'Is this your boy?'

'No, no,' said Munro with a smile. 'This is Detective Sergeant Dougal McCrae. He's leading the investigation into Jessica's death.'

'Are you not a bit young to be a copper?' said Sullivan. 'I thought you had to be an old bastard to be a detective.'

'I'll take that as a compliment,' said Munro. 'Will we step inside?'

'We will not. We'll stop right here. I'll give you five minutes.'

'But it's freezing,' said Dougal. 'You'll catch your death.'

'Have no fear. I'm harder than a Geordie, son. Five minutes.'

'Okay, your car…'

'It's not here. The police took it.'

'Can you confirm the make and model?'

'Vauxhall Insignia. SA16 OCG.'

'And last night, who was driving it?'

'Not me,' said Sullivan. 'I'd had a skinful.'

'A quiet night in then, was it?'

'Poldark, a curry, and a bottle of Buckfast.'

'If you were here all night, Mrs Sullivan…'

'It's Miss.'

'…then why did you not answer when the police knocked your door?'

'I must've been sleeping. Buckfast, it has that effect.'

'Fair enough,' said Dougal. 'Can you tell me if anyone else is insured to drive your car?'

'No. Just me.'

'Could anyone have taken it without your consent?'

'You mean like some ned off on a joyride?'

'Actually,' said Munro, his eyes narrowing, 'we were thinking more along the lines of Alessandro Ricci.'

Sullivan lit her cigarette, drew hard, and blew a pall of smoke into the air.

'You'd best come in,' she said. 'You've a minute left.'

Munro, expecting the interior of the house to reflect its period status, entered the lounge and cringed at the two faux-leather sofas positioned to face a forty-eight-inch television set hanging above an original Adams fireplace, a potted, plastic palm, and a bookcase doubling as a storage facility for dirty crockery and takeaway cartons.

Sullivan slumped on the settee, lit another cigarette and crossed her legs while Dougal and Munro remained standing by the door.

'So,' said Munro. 'Alessandro Ricci. You first.'

'He prefers Alex.'

'You say he rents a room,' said Dougal. 'So he's your lodger?'

Sullivan glanced furtively at Munro, blushed, and stubbed out the cigarette.

'See here, Miss Sullivan,' he said. 'The average life expectancy in these parts is seventy-one years for someone like myself which means it'll not be long before they measure me for a box, so, if it's all the same with you, I'd rather not waste my time. You can either answer the question honestly or…'

'Or I'll arrest you,' said Dougal chipping in, 'on suspicion of being an accessory after the fact.'

'What the hell does that mean?'

'I'll explain at the station. If you'd like to get dressed, I've a couple of officers waiting for you outside.'

'Okay look,' said Sullivan, 'he doesn't rent a room. He's with me.'

'And how long have you been together?'

'Not long. A couple of months.'

'How did you meet?'

'He dropped by the shop.'

'Shop?'

'The estate agents where I work. He was after some office space.'

'And did he get it?'

'He did, aye.'

'Whereabouts?'

'Titchfield Street,' said Sullivan. 'Number fifty-five.'

'Is he there now?'

'He should be.'

'So, back to the original question,' said Dougal. 'Your car. Could Mr Ricci have taken it without your consent?'

'He doesn't have to ask. He can use it whenever he likes.'

'And how does that work? I mean, if he wants to borrow it and you're not here?'

'I've a spare key hidden away.'

'Whereabouts?'

'If I told you that,' said Sullivan, 'it wouldn't be hidden, would it?'

'Aye, right enough,' said Dougal. 'So, I assume if Mr Ricci's taking advantage of your generosity then, naturally, you have him down as a nominated driver on your insurance?'

Sullivan said nothing and turned to face the window.

'Dear, dear, dear,' said Munro, smiling as he shook his head. 'If he's not insured then unless I'm mistaken that's a five thousand pound fine and six points on the licence. I'm assuming he does have a licence?'

'Okay, here's the deal,' said Dougal, 'we're away to see Mr Ricci just now and I'd advise you against calling him and giving him the heads-up because if he's not there when we arrive, I'll make sure you're prosecuted for allowing him to drive your car without adequate cover.'

'Big deal,' said Sullivan. 'So what? I'll get a wee slap on the wrist and...'

'No, no, no. You'll be liable for the same penalty.'

'Are you joking me? Five grand? Why?'

'Because it's your responsibility to ensure anyone you lend your car to holds a full licence and is properly insured. It's what the law deems "an absolute offence" which means no excuses. If you're guilty, then you will be fined as well.'

'And dinnae forget the bonus points,' said Munro, 'they all add up. Before we go, I appreciate we're into extra time but we've a couple more questions.'

'In for a penny,' said Sullivan. 'On you go.'

'Jessica. Your estranged daughter. Did she have trouble sleeping?'

'I've no idea. She'd be out when most folk were in their beds. She'd roll in during the wee small hours and sleep while I was at work.'

'So, you've no idea if she was on any kind of medication? Sleeping pills?'

'No.'

'She and Mr Ricci,' said Dougal. 'Did they get along?'

'What do you mean?'

'Just that. How was their relationship?'

'Relationship?' said Sullivan indignantly. 'Here you, are you suggesting that she and...'

'Calm yourself, Miss Sullivan, I'm suggesting nothing. I'd simply like to know if there was any animosity between them. It's not uncommon, a mother gets a new boyfriend, the daughter gets upset...'

'They got along just fine.'

'Is that so?'

'Aye,' said Sullivan. 'It is. They'd even go for coffee together, or a wee drink if I was late getting back.'

'So, they were close?'

'Close? Listen son, I'm not happy with what you're insinuating, in fact I just might…'

'In that case,' said Munro, 'we'll leave you be. And remember, Miss Sullivan, if you telephone Mr Ricci it'll be the most expensive call you've ever made. Cheery-bye.'

* * *

Standing in the shabby surroundings of his small, unfurnished office located above a wholesaler specialising in liquidated stock, Alessandro Ricci – dressed in a beige linen suit and a white open-necked shirt – cut an incongruous figure as he gazed from the window at the queue of traffic below, unaware of the two gentlemen hovering by the open doorway.

Dougal rapped the door and coughed politely into his hand.

'Alessandro Ricci?' he said, waving his warrant card.

Ricci cocked his head, smiled softly, and nodded.

'I'm Detective Sergeant McCrae and this is Mr Munro. Would you mind if we asked you a few questions?'

'Please,' said Ricci with a sweep of the arm, 'come in. I'd offer you a seat but as you can see…'

Munro cast an eye around the spartan room; the bare walls, the empty table, and the single chair.

'You've not quite moved in then?' he said.

'I have all I need.'

'But you've not even got yourself a telephone.'

'I don't need one,' said Ricci as he produced his mobile. 'I can do everything on this.'

'Then why do you need an office?'

'I need space to think, Mr Munro. Somewhere I can be alone without interruptions or distractions.'

'I see,' said Munro. 'Tell me, what line of business is it that you're in exactly?'

'Anything that is legal and turns a profit.'

'I'm glad to see capitalism's alive and well in Siena,' said Dougal.

Ricci raised his eyebrows and smiled.

'You've done your research, Sergeant. I'm impressed. So, what can I help you with?'

'Let's start with Helen Sullivan.'

'Ah! Bellissima! She will make somebody a wonderful wife.'

'But not you?'

'I'm too old for commitment. I am an ambassador for la dolce vita.'

'Have you not heard of growing old gracefully?'

'There is nothing graceful about growing old. Trust me.'

'So,' said Dougal, 'you and Miss Sullivan. How did you meet?'

'I was looking for an office and she found me this.'

'Forgive me for saying so,' said Munro, 'but it doesnae seem to go with your image.'

'I wanted somewhere, how can I say…'

'Low key?'

'Yes. Exactly.'

'You sound as though you're trying to keep your head down.'

'I walk with my head held high,' said Ricci. 'I am a proud man.'

'Good for you,' said Dougal. 'Would you mind telling me just how long you've been living with Miss Sullivan?'

'Eight weeks. In fact, eight weeks and three days to be precise.'

'You must like her to remember that.'

'I have a head for figures.'

'I bet you have,' said Munro muttering under his breath. 'Miss Sullivan's daughter, Jessica…'

'Such a tragedy.'

'Were you fond of her?'

'Fond? That's a rather odd word to use.'

'I'll ask again. Were you fond of her?'

'I liked her, yes. She was good company.'

'Miss Sullivan says that you and Jessica used to hang out together,' said Dougal, 'go for the occasional coffee, a wee drink, that sort of thing.'

'We did, Sergeant. Quite often in fact.'

'Did the two of you ever get... close?'

'Close?' said Ricci. 'You mean intimate? Come, come, she was just a child. There are some lines a gentleman does not cross.'

Munro, hands clasped behind his back, raised his head to the ceiling and chuckled softly.

'Have you ever done any acting, Mr Ricci?' he said. 'In the theatre perhaps?'

'No, why do you ask?'

'Because I'm watching one hell of a performance just now. Tell me, when was the last time you used Miss Sullivan's motor car?'

'Yesterday.'

'And are you insured to drive it?'

'Of course I am,' said Ricci. 'Helen took care of that.'

'Did she indeed. And where did you go?'

'I had two appointments. First I went to visit a restaurant looking for investors and then I had a meeting with a trading standards advisor at the civic centre.'

'Trading standards?'

'I wanted to clarify my legal obligations for importing wine.'

'Another business opportunity?'

'Another business possibility. I have a vineyard in Tuscany.'

'I'm not averse to a decent drop of red myself,' said Munro. 'So you're thinking of selling your wine here?'

'As I said, it's a possibility.'

'And where would you sell it? The supermarkets maybe? Or the nightclubs? Bakers nightclub perhaps?'

Ricci, toying with the gold signet ring on his little finger, leaned against the window and smiled.

'You know something,' he said, 'it's a good job I'm not paranoid or I might think you've been following me.'

'Can you explain what you were doing there?' said Dougal.

'Jessica. She telephoned me. She said she couldn't get a taxi and asked if I would pick her up.'

'Would you mind if we checked your phone?'

'I have nothing to hide, Sergeant,' said Ricci as he handed it over. 'If it's proof you're after, you'll find it right there.'

Knowing that there was no feasible way of falsifying an incoming call unless he was in possession of Jessica's handset, Dougal, already frustrated by Ricci's candour, checked the log, the date, and the time and reluctantly returned it with his business card.

'A wee favour, Mr Ricci,' he said. 'Would you mind dialling that number for me then hanging up?'

'Why?'

'So I'll have your number. Just in case I need to get in touch.'

'Jessica went to the club with her friend,' said Munro. 'Sophie Jackson. Did you not pick her up too?'

'No,' said Ricci. 'She refused to come with me.'

'And why was that?'

'I have no idea. I got the impression they had been arguing but I may be wrong.'

'And why did you not take Jessica home?'

'She said she felt queasy, light-headed. She asked me to drop her off so she could get some air.'

'At that time of night?' said Dougal. 'In this weather?'

'I am used to the sunshine, Sergeant. I simply assumed her behaviour was typical of those who live in arctic conditions.'

'But you didn't think to follow her? Or wait for her?'

'No. Was that so wrong?'

Munro glowered at Ricci, folded his arms and, with one hand on his chin, stifled a yawn.

'You are tired, Mr Munro?'

'It's been a long night.'

'And you have trouble sleeping?'

'Insomnia,' said Munro facetiously. 'I should take a wee pill but the trouble with that is, you lose control of your senses.'

'Did you know that the main cause of insomnia is not stress or over-work but a guilty conscience?'

'Is that so?'

'It is,' said Ricci. 'The subconscious can play havoc when the mind is at rest. Personally, I never have any trouble sleeping.'

'Then you're a lucky man,' said Dougal. 'Are you enjoying it here in Scotland, Mr Ricci?'

Ricci thought for a moment, slipped his hands into pockets, pursed his lips and then shrugged his shoulders.

'I think so,' he said. 'It's… different.'

'And have you done much sightseeing since you've been here?'

'A little. The local area.'

'So, did you enjoy your trip to Arran?'

'I'm sorry,' said Ricci. 'Arran?'

'The Isle of Arran. You can see it from here.'

'I'm afraid I've never been.'

'Well that is odd,' said Dougal, 'because Miss Sullivan's car was on the ferry from Ardrossan to Brodick.'

'Then perhaps it was *Miss Sullivan* who took it.'

Munro walked to the chipped, Formica-topped table, rubbed his chest, and perched on the edge.

'Ella MacCall,' he said. 'Tell me about her.'

Showing the first signs of nervousness, Ricci glanced out of the window, cleared his throat and ran his fingers through his hair.

'She's a very talented lady,' he said.

'How so?'

'You're not familiar with her work? I think she is destined for great things. Her films are reminiscent of a young Visconti, you know, *Ossessione*, *Death in Venice*?'

'So, you like your films?'

'We Italians are masters of the cinema, Mr Munro. It is one of my passions.'

'Do you enjoy literature too? Reading, I mean?'

'I do.'

'Newspapers?'

'News is depressing.'

'Nick Riley,' said Dougal chipping in. 'Do you recognise the name?'

'Should I?'

'He's a journalist.'

'I don't know him.'

'He knows you.'

'I'm flattered.'

'Can you vouch for your whereabouts over the last couple of days?'

'Questo è impossibile, amico mio,' said Ricci, shaking his head. 'I am a busy man.'

'Okay,' said Dougal, 'I'll take that as a no then. I think we're almost done here but I'd just like to check; you're not planning on leaving the country any time soon, are you?'

'And why would I do that?'

'Old habits,' said Munro, 'die hard.'

'I can assure you, Mr Munro, I have no intention of…'

'See here, Mr Ricci,' said Dougal, scratching the back of his head, 'I'm afraid that's a risk I'm just not willing to take. Alessandro Ricci, I'm arresting you on suspicion of causing grievous bodily harm, oh, and driving without insurance. You do not have to say anything but it may harm your defence if you do not mention when questioned something you later rely on in court. Anything you do say may be given in evidence. Do you understand?'

Chapter 9

Reaching for his shades as the dappled sunlight played on his face like a strobe in a discotheque, Duncan – bouncing in his seat like a co-driver in the Scottish Rally Championship – tried his best to remain calm as West floored the Defender, bombing through the wooded countryside dodging red squirrels and the occasional hare before slowing to a crawl around Lamlash Bay and yelping with delight at the unfettered view of the mainland shimmering in the distance.

'Look at that!' she said. 'It's stunning! The scenery around here is bleeding stunning!'

'Miss, are you familiar with the phrase "speed kills"?'

'So do most amphetamines,' said West. 'Stop worrying, you're in safe hands.'

* * *

The antiquated appearance of McIver's garage, reminiscent of an age when the roads were populated with Model Ts and Austin 7s was, to an outsider, the kind of place where terms like "diagnostics", "emissions", and "traction control" were bandied about with derision and any vehicle which couldn't be started with a crank handle would be turned away.

West parked on the forecourt alongside a redundant petrol pump, grinning as she pointed out the mud-encrusted Land Cruiser.

'That must be his,' she said.

'How so?'

'The number plate, dopey. SN54 RSQ.'

'Sorry?'

'RSQ. Rescue.'

'Oh, very clever,' said Duncan sardonically. 'Very clever indeed.'

* * *

Dressed in dark blue overalls with a tweed cap sitting on the back of his head, McIver, fastidiously decoking an alloy cylinder head, looked up from his workbench roused by the sight of a lithesome West in her black jeans, white T-shirt and a Belstaff jacket swanning through the door with her hands on her hips. Downing tools, he rubbed the greying stubble on his chin and smiled as she sauntered towards him.

'John McIver?' she said, waving her warrant card.

'At your service.'

'DI West. And this is DC Reid.'

'You're here about the girl?'

'Ella MacCall. That's right. Have you got a minute?'

'I've got as long as you like.'

Duncan rolled his eyes and perched on an empty oil drum while West, enamoured of the anomalous array of hi-tech equipment, outboard motors, a quad bike, and a spanking new Range Rover straddling the service pit, wandered aimlessly around the workshop like a tourist in an art gallery.

'Can you run me through what happened that night?' she said.

'Have you not spoken with Bobby?'

'PC Mackenzie? Yeah, we have. Diamond bloke, very helpful but I'd like to hear it from you.'

'Well I'm not sure what else I can tell you,' said McIver. 'We got the call-out, headed up the fell, and thanks to Bailey…'

'Bailey? He didn't mention him. Is he one of your team?'

'Oh aye. He's the most valuable member we've got. He's a retriever.'

'Ah, lovely! Sorry, go on.'

'If it wasn't for him, I doubt we'd have found her. It pains me to say it but we were too late, so down we came and off she went.'

'Did she have any injuries?'

'Aye, she did,' said McIver. 'A broken leg and a wee cut to the head but ultimately it was the cold that took her. She had severe frostbite, which is no surprise, and visibility was zero. Chances are she lost her footing, slipped and fell.'

'Mackenzie said you were quite peeved that night. Understandably so given what you'd been through.'

'Peeved? No, no,' said McIver. 'I was raging. It's not often we get a fatality and it's not the fact that she went up there ill-equipped and under-dressed, it's the fact that her so-called friends did nothing to stop her.'

'For what it's worth,' said Duncan, 'they did try. Apparently.'

'Well, not hard enough. Not in my book. She should have been forcibly restrained.'

West slipped her hands into her pockets, leaned against the bench, and shot him a sympathetic smile.

'It can't be easy doing what you do,' she said. 'This sort of thing obviously hits you where it hurts.'

'No, Inspector. I'm too long in the tooth for that. It's stupidity and a lack of loyalty that hits me where it hurts.'

'Silly question, I know,' said West, 'but did you find anything up there?'

'We're always finding stuff up there. You'll not believe what these nature-loving walkers and climbers leave behind.'

'Like what?'

'Rubbish,' said McIver. 'What's left of their packed lunches, spent batteries, anything they can't be arsed to carry back with them.'

'And that night?'

'Och, you'll have to ask Isla, she's like a magpie when it comes to picking up litter.'

'Sorry, Isla?'

'Isla Thomson. She's one of us and my number two when we're on a shout. Hold on, I'll fetch her.'

McIver wandered to the rear of the garage and disappeared through the back door while West, peering through the window of the Range Rover, sneered at what she considered to be the car of choice for footballers and drug dealers.

'What do you reckon, miss?' said Duncan as he polished his shades.

'I prefer my Defender.'

'No, I meant McIver.'

'Seems like a nice bloke.'

'He's an eye for yourself.'

'Behave,' said West. 'What about you? What do you think?'

'If I'm honest,' said Duncan, 'the way I see it, anyone who's willing to risk their own life to save some numpty deserves a slap on the back in my book. Hats off to the fella.'

* * *

'Inspector!' said McIver, yelling as he returned from the yard. 'This is Isla. Isla, Inspector West and… sorry son, I can't remember your…'

'No bother,' said Duncan. 'It's not important.'

'Nice to meet you,' said West. 'Mr McIver was just telling us that you're his second in command.'

'Aye, and the rest.'

'Come again?'

'Second in command, dietician, diary. This fella would be lost if I didn't keep him in check.'

'So you work here too?'

'No, no,' said Isla. 'I'm a teacher, Brodick Primary. I've a wee while before class so I said I'd clear out the Cat before John gives it a service.'

'The cat?'

'The Argo Cat. It's our ATV, an eight-wheeler. It gets us pretty much anywhere we need to go. So, how can I help?'

'We were just talking about Ella MacCall.'

'Oh aye, poor girl. Such a needless waste of life.'

'And I was wondering,' said West, 'I know conditions were bad up there but did you happen to find anything?'

'I'm not with you.'

'Anything someone might have lost or thrown away. I dunno, like a phone maybe, or gloves, that sort of thing.'

'No,' said Isla as she plonked a carrier bag on the bench, 'not at the top, but these are the bits and bobs I collected as we came down. There's not much there but help yourself.'

West snapped on a pair of gloves, rolled down the bag, and rummaged through the contents.

'Beggars belief,' she said as she pulled out two empty cans of lager, a comb, a silver flask, a scarf and an empty sandwich wrapper. 'Litter louts, they get my back up.'

'That makes two of us.'

'Whoever had this must've liked their brew,' said West as she shook the flask, 'it's almost empty.'

'And it's brand new,' said Isla. 'It's yours if you want it.'

'No ta, got one. Maybe the charity shop will take it.'

'Aye, probably. I'll drop it in once I've given it a wee rinse. Well, that's me, wouldn't do for the teacher to be late now, would it?'

'Right enough,' said McIver. 'Thanks doll, are you up for a wee bevvy later? My treat.'

'Okay, you're on. Would you care to join us, Inspector?'

'Thanks,' said West, 'but we need to head back soon.'

'Oh, hold on,' said Duncan, leaping from his seat. 'Sorry, Miss Thomson, but where did you say you found that flask?'

'A couple of miles up the path.'

'And this path, would it be the same path the walkers would use if they were heading up Goat Fell?'

'Aye, indeed it would.'

Duncan turned to West and frowned as he lowered his voice.

'That Megan Dalgleish,' he said. 'She told us Ella went up there with a flask and a packet of crisps. Is it not worth a punt?'

'Bloody well is,' said West as she grabbed the bag. 'We'll take it after all. In fact, we'll take the whole lot.'

* * *

Seemingly preoccupied, West slipped the key into the ignition, slumped in her seat and stared at the Land Cruiser.

'Are we okay for time?' she said.

'Aye,' said Duncan, buttoning his coat, 'which makes me wonder…'

'What?'

'Well as we're here and McIver's a mechanic, maybe he could take a look at the heater. It's like an igloo in here.'

'Nonsense,' said West, 'it's not cold, it's fresh, that's all. It helps to keep your wits about you.'

'It's not my wits I'm worried about.'

'Okay, listen up. As soon as we get back, I want you to run this bag of toot up to forensic services for analysis.'

'Forensics? In Glasgow?'

'Yup. It won't take you long from Ardrossan, you can drive this and I'll get Dougal to sort me out a lift. I want prints and DNA off everything and I want to know what's in that flask apart from tea, understood?'

'Roger that, miss.'

'And if they give you any grief about getting it done, call me and I'll give them a boot up the backside. We need results back quick-sticks, oh, and while you're waiting, give McLeod a bell, ask him to send MacCall's DNA to FS for a possible match.'

'No bother.'

Aware that West's catalogue of facial expressions was limited to wooden and deadpan unless cracking a joke, Duncan – conscious of the sudden dip in her enthusiasm – had nonetheless learned to recognise when her inscrutable gaze was the result of something deeper.

'What's up?' he said.

West fumbled in her pockets and retrieved two crumpled sheets of paper, smoothed them on her lap, and began reading.

'Dunno,' she said. 'It just seems familiar, that's all.'

'What does?'

'That number plate. RSQ.'

'It would. You clocked it when we came in.'

West thrust the sheets of paper into Duncan's chest and leapt from the car.

'I knew it,' she said. 'Sit tight. Back in a jiff.'

* * *

McIver, still busying himself with the cylinder head, looked up and winked at West.

'Don't tell me,' he said, 'you've changed your mind about tonight?'

'Fat chance,' said West. 'The Cruiser out front...'

'Oh, it's not for sale. It's mine.'

'Thought so. Can you tell me what you were doing on the 6:55 ferry from Ardrossan?'

'Am I under suspicion, Inspector? Because if you want to take me in, I'll not put up a fight.'

'In your dreams. So?'

'TMS Spares,' said McIver. 'North Harbour Industrial Estate. I was picking up stock. Brake pads, cables, hoses, everyday stuff.'

'Can you prove it?'

'You're not one for trusting folk, are you Inspector? I'll fetch the invoice, it'll have the date and the time on it.'

'Cheers. And after that, what did you do?'

'I unloaded here,' said McIver as West pulled her phone from her hip and took a snap of the receipt, 'then I made a dash for the doctor because I was on-call from eight. It was all a bit rushed.'

'The doctor? Cripes, sorry,' said West, 'I didn't realise you were ill.'

'You're alright, I'm not ill. I had to fetch my prescription, that's all.'

'Still, nothing serious I hope.'

'No, no. Just my sleeping pills. Sometimes I need them when I'm not on duty.'

'I don't blame you,' said West. 'Thanks again, I'll leave you in peace now, I really have to… hold up, did you say sleeping pills?'

'I did, aye.'

'Your GP, is he nearby?'

'Sorry, Inspector, but why is that of interest to you?'

'Just wondering.'

'Are you indeed? Follow the shore road, you'll find the surgery right next to the coastguard station.'

* * *

Despite the dazzling sunshine, the medical centre – a drab pebble-dashed bungalow with faded paintwork and lifeless windows – remained as grey and foreboding as a storm surge in the Firth of Clyde.

'Now this,' said Duncan, 'is the kind of place where you'd wipe your feet on the way out. I'm not touching anything.'

Assuming the lack of response was down to nothing more than a faulty bell, West – employing the kind of tactics normally reserved for shaking villains from their slumber at four o'clock in the morning – hammered the door with the side of her fist with a vociferous request to "open up" only to be greeted seconds later by a disgruntled receptionist wearing the sanctimonious smile of an air hostess on a charter flight to Benidorm.

Regarding Duncan as if he'd been hauled off the streets by a social worker, she turned to face West and huffed.

'Consultations are by appointment only,' she said.

West produced her warrant card and held it an inch from her face.

'I don't think we need one,' she said. 'Can we come in?'

* * *

Doctor Audra Shea, a plump fifty-something with a rosy complexion who needed to heed her own advice when it came to recommending the benefits of healthy eating and limiting alcohol consumption, struggled to budge from her chair and chose to remain seated instead.

'And a good morning to you,' she said as the surly receptionist left the room. 'How can I help?'

'I'm Detective Inspector West and this is DC Reid.'

'Are you here on business?' she asked, making a laboured point of eyeing Duncan from head to toe, 'or is it something of a personal nature?'

'Oh, good grief,' said West. 'We're here about John McIver.'

'John? Oh my, whatever is the matter?'

'Calm yourself, hen,' said Duncan, 'he's fine, toiling away in his wee garage.'

'Then?'

'He says he gets his sleeping pills from you. Is that so?'

'I couldn't say,' said Shea. 'Sorry. Client confidentiality.'

'See here, doctor, your client has already told us that he does get his tablets here, therefore that information is no longer confidential, do you get what I'm saying?'

'Aye, but that's not how it works.'

'We just want to know what tablets he's taking,' said West. 'Whether it's lightweight stuff you can get over the counter or something stronger?'

'Well, why can't you ask him yourself?'

'Because we don't want him to know.'

'Why ever not?'

'Can't say,' said West. 'It's confidential.'

'No, I'm sorry, I'd like to help but…'

'Okay,' said West. 'No sweat, I'll put in an official request. I just have to nip back to the station and sort the paperwork. DC Reid can wait here.'

'As you wish.'

'With any luck,' said West glancing at her watch, 'I should be back in about four hours. Might take a bit longer.'

Shea, flabbergasted, glanced at Duncan and winced.

'Four hours you say? That's an awful waste of time. Let me see what I can do.'

Shea reached for her spectacles, logged into her computer and, using her two index fingers, slowly searched for McIver's records.

'Okey-dokey,' she said, 'We started him off on a ten-milligram dose of Diphenhydramine Hydrochloride, it's basically an antihistamine which gets you drowsy but that didn't work for him, so we upped it to twenty-five.'

'And that's something you can get anywhere?'

'Aye, any pharmacy will have them.'

'But?'

'But that didn't work either. Ever since then he's been on Flunitrazepam. They are prescription only.'

'So they'd knock you for a six?' said Duncan.

'In a manner of speaking. He's on a low dose mind, one milligram, not to be taken regularly, just as and when.'

'And how many does he get?' said West.

'Each box contains thirty tablets. That normally sees him right for about three months.'

'This fluni...'

'Flunitrazepam.'

'Aye. Flunitrazepam,' said Duncan. 'Does it come by any other name? You know, like a brand or something?'

'It does. It's called Rohypnol.'

Chapter 10

Declining his request for a small glass of Cinzano Rosso and a plate of crostini, Dougal – in a rare display of churlish cynicism – led Ricci to his cell, pointed out the en-suite facilities and apologised for the lack of bed linen, Wi-Fi, and a mini bar before leaving him alone to run a cross-check on his fingerprints while Munro, frustrated by his sudden inability to dash up the four flights of stairs, made his way slowly to the top floor, drew a deep breath, and ambled into DCI Elliot's office.

'James! I've not seen you in days! Where the devil have you been?'

'Och, here and there,' said Munro. 'Am I interrupting anything?'

'No, no. It's just admin.'

'Admin? Are you joking me? You're not one for paperwork, George, what's the story?'

'This paperwork,' said Elliot, 'is different.'

'How so?'

'Two boarding passes for a flight to Dublin.'

'Not the fair city where the girls are so pretty?'

'The same.'

'Another holiday?'

'A weekend away.'

'You're all heart,' said Munro, 'but I cannae make it, I've some decorating to finish.'

'Another time, then.'

'So, what's the occasion?'

'Anniversary.'

'But it's not your anniversary for months.'

'It's the anniversary of the day Mrs Elliot threatened to leave me unless I took her on a wee break.'

'And when was that?'

'Two days ago,' said Elliot. 'So, tell me, what's bothering you?'

'Nothing at all,' said Munro as he produced an envelope from his jacket pocket and handed it over. 'A wee favour is all. I wonder if you'd be kind enough to witness this for me. I've not had a chance to type it up yet but I thought I could leave that to the solicitor.'

'Solicitor?' said Elliot. 'This all sounds very formal, James, what is it? A letter of… good heavens man! It's a last will and testament!'

'Correct.'

'What's going on? Are you not telling me something?'

'Like what?'

'I'm not sure. I mean, you're not…?'

'Dead? No, not yet,' said Munro. 'I'm just getting my house in order. I've been meaning to do it ever since Jean passed on but I've not had the chance. Until now.'

'There's something macabre about this.'

'You should do one yourself, George…'

'They're not planting me just yet.'

'…or Mrs Elliot will get the lot.'

'I have to admit,' said Elliot, 'you've a point there, James. You certainly have a point. Should I read this or is it personal?'

'On you go, there's no surprises.'

Elliot, holding a superstitious belief that being privy to such information might tempt the hand of fate and cause his friend to expire on the spot, took a hesitant breath, read the first of four hand-written pages penned in a deep blue ink and glanced at Munro.

'I've not seen my name yet, James,' he said. 'I hope it's not here.'

'No, no. You're the last person I'd want to embarrass with material gain, George.'

'Thanking you.'

'Instead, I shall bequeath you my cheerful disposition.'

'Very kind, I'm sure.'

'You know me, I'm not happy unless I'm miserable.'

Elliot turned the page, read the first paragraph and smiled.

'You always were generous, James,' he said, 'but this? Your house?'

'Well, I'd rather it went to someone who'll care for it the way Jean and myself have done over the years, otherwise what will happen? It'll pass to the crown, *bona vacantia*, and be sold off for two and six.'

'Does she know about this?'

'Charlie? Of course not,' said Munro. 'And she's not to find out either, do I make myself clear?'

'You have my word.'

Elliot reached for his fountain pen, signed his name alongside Munro's and just for good measure, rubber-stamped it with the date.

'Nothing against Charlie,' he said, 'but I hope to God she doesn't get her hands on that house for at least another twenty years.'

'You and me both, George,' said Munro. 'You and me both.'

* * *

Whilst keen to uncover anything that might incriminate Alessandro Ricci on a charge of assault or justify Ella MacCall's irrational desire to scale Arran's tallest peak, Dougal – compelled to sate a burgeoning appetite –

suspended his search of social media, school records, and news articles to order lunch just as Munro, desperate to put his feet up before heading to the solicitor's office, shuffled wearily through the door and sat down.

'Jeez-oh, don't take this the wrong way, boss, but you're looking a wee bit puggled.'

'Well, it's no surprise,' said Munro, 'I was up all night, I've not slept, and I've hardly eaten.'

'You'll be needing a brew then.'

'Thanking you.'

'And no doubt you're hungry?'

'Like it's the last day of Lent.'

'Good,' said Dougal, 'because lunch is on its way. You can choose between a pizza or a ham and cheese toastie.'

'What's on the pizza?'

'Pepperoni and chillies.'

'I'll take the toastie. So, how's our Italian friend?'

'Well, he's not happy about having to give up his belt and his jewellery and he's not impressed with room service either. He ordered a cocktail.'

'Is it not a bit early to be hitting the sauce?'

'Actually, he called it an aperitif.'

'He would,' said Munro. 'Let's hope he's not got any health problems, it wouldnae do for him to keel over in custody.'

'Not much chance of that boss. He's registered at the Carrick Glen hospital. It's private.'

'Well, at least he's not here to sponge off the NHS. No doubt his lawyer's already on the way over.'

'No, no,' said Dougal. 'Get this, he's refused any kind of legal representation.'

'Really? Why so?'

'He says he's no faith in the judicial system and if he has to, he'd rather defend himself.'

'More fool him,' said Munro. 'He'll be like a lamb to the slaughter. What else?'

'He's matched positive for the prints off Sullivan's motor.'

'Well, that's a given, he's already admitted taking it.'

'So I'm holding him until the DI gets back, she needs a word. Apparently, he and Ella MacCall were involved.'

'Involved with what?'

'Each other.'

'Are you joking me?' said Munro, his lip curling with disgust. 'A man of his age? Dear, dear, dear. Is he aware of the fact that you know of their relationship?'

'No, boss. I'm leaving that bombshell for West.'

'Wise move, laddie. It doesnae do to show your hand all at once.'

'And when she's done with him, I'll do him for driving with no insurance.'

'And Miss Sullivan?'

'I'll not charge her just yet. Not unless she slips up.'

'Instinct tells me she's a step away from a banana skin.'

'How so?'

'Och, come on Dougal,' said Munro, 'you're a clever lad, you've a great career ahead of you but as I've said to Charlie, if you're going to get on then there are times when you need to step away from the facts and start listening to your gut.'

'I'm not with you, boss.'

'Read between the lines. Ricci marches into her office looking for business premises and in no time at all they're co-habiting.'

'Aye, it happens.'

'Why? Why was he so keen to move in with her?'

'Maybe she wanted him to.'

'Or maybe it's because he didnae have a permanent address. Do your research, laddie. If I'm right he'd have been laid up in a hotel or a bed and breakfast. One thing's for sure, he's with her for a reason and it's nothing to do with love.'

'So, what you're saying is, this happy-family thing is some kind of a charade? A front? A cover for something else?'

'That's exactly what I'm saying,' said Munro. 'I'll not be surprised if he's got something on her and he's using her as an alibi for his shenanigans.'

'Aye, you could be right.'

'I'm not finished yet. A couple of months after moving in with Sullivan, her daughter winds up dead yet she's as cold as a block of ice. Does that not strike you as a wee bit odd?'

'In all fairness,' said Dougal, 'she said they didn't get along.'

'By jiminy!' said Munro. 'It's her daughter we're talking about! Her own flesh and blood! Where's the remorse? See here, if they didnae get along then young Jessica would have moved out months ago! No, no, you mark my words, there's something not quite right there. Not right at all.'

'And there was I thinking she'd been quite sincere.'

'Two words laddie: book and cover. Now, where's Charlie? Is she turning her wee trip into a six-month sabbatical?'

'She's on her way,' said Dougal. 'Duncan's taking her car up to FS in Glasgow to get some evidence tested so I have to arrange a pick-up for her. I'd go on my scooter but I'm not sure she'd be happy with that.'

'You'd be surprised. Not too long ago she was galavanting around on the back of a Harley.'

'Jeez-oh! You're right! Maybe I should go after all.'

'You stay here,' said Munro. 'If there's one thing I have in spades just now, Dougal, it's time. I'll take care of it.'

* * *

With his coat zipped to the neck and his thinning, grey hair blowing in the breeze, Munro – clutching a white piece of card emblazoned with the word "West" – watched as a steady stream of passengers spilled from the ferry onto the quayside until a bewildered-looking West, the last to disembark, finally caught his eye and skipped towards him like a long-lost relative returning to the homeland.

'There has to be a better way of supplementing your pension Jimbo!' she said, grinning as she gave him a hug.

'Please, Charlie, a handshake will do.'

'Oh, stop being such a sourpuss! What's up? You're looking peaky.'

'Not you as well,' said Munro as he led her to the car. 'I've not slept, that's all.'

'Oh cripes, sorry I forgot. How is she? Your mate's daughter?'

'Och, she'll be fine. She's just a wee bit shaken, that's all.'

'And the Sullivan girl? Is Dougal on the case?'

'Aye, he's like a dog with a bone,' said Munro, 'but a word to the wise, lassie, the poor lad's going to need some time off before he has a breakdown, he's fair worn out having to deal with her and this Ricci character, not to mention the fellow who was stabbed on Sandgate.'

'Relax Jimbo, he thrives on it,' said West, 'he just needs to loosen up, get out a bit more.'

'You know as well as I do, Charlie, when it comes to social animals, Dougal's something of a sloth.'

'Okay, point taken. I'll pack him off on a fishing trip once we're done. Anyway, how about you? What's the score?'

'Baneshanks 1 – Longevity 0.'

Not wishing to show her ignorance regarding the Angel of Death West, assuming that Baneshanks played centre-forward for Celtic FC, settled down to enjoy the half hour jaunt back to the office while a melancholy Munro, pootling along at a steady forty, made a point of soaking up the scenery.

'So, tell me, Charlie, did you enjoy your trip?'

'Yeah, as it happens, I did,' said West. 'Tell you what though, it's a shame we couldn't have stayed a bit longer. I wouldn't have minded a trek up that Goat Fell myself.'

'Well, as they say across the water, you've got to go to come.'

'You what?'

'Never mind. How's your investigation coming along?'

'Oh please, not now, Jimbo,' said West. 'Can we talk shop later? What've you been up to?'

'Och, nothing new,' said Munro. 'I was throwing some paint at the kitchen when Paul Jackson telephoned to ask if I'd help locate his daughter.'

'Well it's a bloody good job you did otherwise we'd have…'

'That's exactly what I said to Dougal. Apart from that I've nothing to report. And yourself?'

'Shattered,' said West. 'What I need is a quiet night in, some decent grub and a bottomless bottle of red.'

'You're beginning to sound like somebody else I know.'

'Who's that?'

'Och, just some Luddite with time on his hands.'

'That'll be you then. So, what do you say? Fancy it?'

'Fancy what Charlie?'

'Dinner. You come to mine. I'll cook, you pour.'

'I'm not sure,' said Munro. 'I've the decorating to finish and…'

'Oh come on, I could do with the company. We'll stop at the butcher on the way and get a couple of sirloins, there's some skinny French fries in the freezer and I've even got a Balvenie on the go.'

'In that case,' said Munro, 'I'd be a fool to refuse. You have yourself a deal lassie. You have yourself a deal.'

* * *

Munro glanced fleetingly at West, smiling as he caught a glimpse of Galloways grazing through the hedgerow.

'Tell me, Charlie, the wee house we looked at in Auchencairn, did you ever follow it up?'

'Yeah, sorry Jimbo, after all the trouble you went to, I should've said. It's a bit of a let-down I'm afraid.'

'How so?'

'Don't get me wrong,' said West, 'I loved the place but I got a copy of the home report and it's a no-go. The rafters are riddled with woodworm, the roof leaks, and it's got rising damp. The whole place needs gutting from top to bottom and I can't afford to do that.'

'Never mind,' said Munro, 'it's obviously not meant to be.'

'Yeah but it's a shame really, I'd kill for a nice little house with a garden. The flat's alright but it's not me.'

'Well, never you mind. Something else will turn up, you wait and see. Now, back to business.'

'Do we have to?'

'Aye, we do. Ella MacCall, have you got anywhere?'

'Hold on, Granddad, why the sudden interest in MacCall? Apart from the fact that you're retired, I thought you had your hands full with your mate's daughter.'

'Had,' said Munro. 'Past tense. So, Ella MacCall, she was drugged, am I right?'

'Spot on Sherlock.'

'Sophie and her pal Jessica were drugged too.'

'You are joking, right?'

'I kid you not. Unfortunately for Jessica, may she rest in peace, the dose was fatal.'

'Bleeding hell,' said West, 'so we've got three on our hands? It's turning into a flipping epidemic. Do you reckon they're related?'

'I'd be surprised if they're not,' said Munro. 'Three young girls, all single, all troubled, and all spiked with Rohypnol.'

'Hold on, what do you mean, troubled?'

'Exactly that. Have you seen the films Ella MacCall posted on her Facebook page?'

'Yeah, I mean, no. I mean I haven't seen them but Dougal's filled me in. It sounds like she was suicidal.'

'She looked it, too. Then there's Jessica Sullivan, by all accounts your average happy-go-lucky kind of a girl, then her mother takes a new boyfriend and all of a sudden she's stopping out all night, hanging around with neds and jakeys, and popping pills like they were going out of fashion.'

'Okay, slow down,' said West. 'That's those two but what about Sophie? You've always said how bright she is.'

'Aye, right enough,' said Munro, 'but see here, Charlie, young Sophie's not been right ever since her mother passed on and she doesnae have a very high opinion of herself either. Paul does his best, God knows he's a martyr to her needs but it doesnae help when the few friends she does have ridicule the way she looks.'

'Unforgiveable,' said West, 'bullying, plain and simple, but it does sound to me like their vulnerability could be a common denominator in them being targeted.'

'You're the expert, lassie. In all my years I've never come across a single case of spiking.'

'I have,' said West, 'it's rife down south and in my experience the perp's a chancer, an opportunist. He'll prey on girls who've had one too many or like I say, seem depressed or vulnerable. The only thing that's premeditated about these kinds of attacks is the fact that the perp knows he's going to do it. As far as the victims are concerned, even he doesn't know who it's going to be. He strikes at random, more often than not playing the Good Samaritan with the offer of a lift home.'

'Well, we're not in London now, Charlie. Or Glasgow. Or Liverpool. Or Leeds. And from where I'm standing, I've reason to believe this fellow was no stranger to the girls. He knew them on a personal level.'

'You're talking about Alessandro Ricci, aren't you?'

'I am indeed,' said Munro. 'Apart from the fact that he and Ella MacCall were in a relationship, according to Miss

Sullivan, he and her daughter were, for want of a better word, *close*.'

'No way!' said West. 'You mean he and she were…'

'I cannae say for sure, you'll have to grill Ricci about that.'

'God, the man's a slime ball. Hold on though, if they were close then why did she go off the rails soon after he moved in?'

'There's seven deadly sins, Charlie. Try lust and anger for starters.'

'And Sophie Jackson,' said West. 'I hate to ask, but did he have anything to do with her?'

'If he did,' said Munro, 'I will personally ensure he's boxed up for the crematorium faster than you can say "pass the matches". That aside, she and Jessica were the best of friends, so I'll not rule it out. Not yet. After all, they were together when he went to pick them up from the nightclub.'

'In the Vauxhall?'

'Aye.'

'And that's what's bugging me. We know the car was on the ferry, we know that's how MacCall and her mates got to Arran, but I've been through the inventory and the ticketing records from CalMac and all the paperwork's in MacCall's name.'

'Does she have a licence?'

'Provisional.'

'So it's not out of the realms of possibility then?'

'It is. The car went back on the return leg.'

'Well, Dougal's convinced it was Ricci behind the wheel but he cannae prove it.'

'And there's the rub,' said West. 'I mean, the only other person who could have been driving is that Sullivan woman and that's hardly likely, is it? She doesn't even know the girls.'

West turned to face Munro, took a deep breath, and stared vacuously at the side of his head.

'Thing is,' she said, 'this theory about Ricci. There's a snag.'

'And what's that?'

'There's somebody else in the frame. The bloke who runs the garage in Lamlash, John McIver. He makes regular trips to the mainland and guess what? He's on Rohypnol.'

'Is that not a wee bit circumstantial, lassie?'

'Maybe. But he's also with mountain rescue. If he is the culprit then I'm thinking he could've been watching MacCall and gone after her before the official callout.'

Munro, choosing to savour the spontaneous silence rather than cut it, gazed dead ahead while West, befuddled by the possibility of having to deal with two suspects, ruffled her hair as if it was infested with nits before breaking the quietude with a frustrated groan.

'For crying out loud!' she said. 'Why is it that every case I get involved with when you're around is like trying to solve a Rubik's cube blindfolded? I need to get my act together. Where's Ricci now?'

'In hospitality,' said Munro, 'waiting for his antipasti.'

'Good,' said West, reaching for her phone, 'I need to get McIver over here too. I'll be damned if I'm getting on that ferry again.'

* * *

Bobby Mackenzie – his confidence boosted by his self-proclaimed "invaluable" contribution to a murder inquiry – walked his usual beat along the promenade with the arrogance of a parking attendant in a pay and display, chatting politely with the locals and poking his head into the shops with a reassuring nod, when his already inflated ego was bolstered even further by a familiar name appearing on his phone.

'DI West,' he said. 'I trust you're well?'

'All good, Constable. How about you?'

'Aye, cracking. By the by, I've sent you the CCTV from the car deck of the *Caledonian Isles*, have you seen it?'

'Not yet, what do you reckon?'

'Well, I'm not a detective, miss, but it seems to me whoever was driving that Insignia knew that there were cameras on-board and didn't want to be seen. He has a scarf tied around his face and a hoodie pulled over his head.'

'Can you get a make on his height? Weight? Build?'

'Oh, I couldn't say, he's wrapped up like a Christmas present.'

'No worries,' said West, 'I'll take a look later. Right, my turn, I've got a job for you.'

'Name it and I'll do my best.'

'I need McIver over here for a chat.'

'John?'

'Yes, John. Why so surprised?'

'Well, because it's John,' said Mackenzie. 'Pillar of the community and all that. He'll not have anything to do with this, miss, trust me. He saves lives, he doesn't take them.'

'I'll be the judge of that,' said West, 'so just you pop along and ask him to get his arse over here as soon as he can.'

'With all due respect, miss, it's a long way to go for a social visit.'

'Well if he's not up for it, you'll have to bring him in yourself.'

'As you wish,' said Mackenzie, 'but I can't force him to come, you know that.'

'You can if you arrest him...'

'Arrest him?'

'...on suspicion of possessing a controlled drug with intent. Got it?'

* * *

Munro, spying a café with a reassuringly long queue as they passed through the quiet side of Wallacetown, pulled over while West, agitated by Mackenzie's reluctance to co-operate, heaved a sigh and scrolled through her phone.

'Some people,' she said. 'Honestly, he's a nice enough bloke but he's being a bit protective about his mates. It's like they're closing ranks.'

'Dinnae take it personally, lassie, in a community like that they like to watch each other's backs.'

'If you say so. Right, I've got one more call to make.'

'You do that,' said Munro, 'and I'll fetch you a bite to eat.'

'Duncan, can you hear me?'

'Aye, miss, just about.'

'What the hell is that noise?'

'It's the wind,' said Duncan, 'there's that many holes in this Defender it's like travelling in a cheese grater.'

'Well look, once you're done with FS I need you to stop off in Kilmarnock on the way back.'

'Are you joking me? Have you not seen the time?'

'Stop whinging,' said West, 'it's on the way. I need you to visit the three tearaways.'

'I should've guessed. Is this about them jumping the early ferry instead of checking in with you?'

'Nah, I'm not fussed about that,' said West, 'I need to know who was driving that Insignia.'

'Okay,' said Duncan, 'but could we not get an FLO to ask them? I mean, they might be in shock, and I'm a fella, and they weren't too keen on talking to me when we were there.'

'Just do it. And don't come back unless you've got an answer.'

'Roger that, miss. I'm on my way.'

* * *

West, her eyes as wide as a ravenous cur on the scent of a sausage, tore through the greasy bag as Munro, his nose twitching at the acidic aroma, opened a window in a futile attempt to alleviate the permeating stench of malt vinegar.

'There's a wee pie in there as well,' he said, filching a chip.

'You, Jimbo, are a lifesaver. I don't know what I'd do without you, you know that?'

Chapter 11

With his misanthropic tendencies compounding his innate inability to suffer fools, Dougal – who believed that punctuality was the politeness of kings rather than a virtue of the bored – paused his application for a permit to fish for grayling and pike in the upper reaches of the Annan and begrudgingly mustered a smile as Nick Riley, an old-school hack with a nose for trouble, breezed through the door precisely fifty-three minutes earlier than expected.

'Mr Riley,' he said, riled by the interruption. 'Thanks for coming.'

'No bother, Dougie, I hope…'

'It's DS McCrae. Have yourself a seat, I'll not be long.'

Assuming the diffident but genial DS who'd interviewed him at his hospital bedside was simply having an off day, Riley – one arm in a sling – brushed off the tetchy response, tossed a plastic wallet onto the desk, and ran a hand through his floppy blond hair.

'Okey-dokey,' said Dougal as the ping of his email heralded the arrival of his permit, 'sorry to keep you. How's the arm?'

'Oh, it's fine, just a couple of stitches,' said Riley as he gestured towards the sling. 'To be honest, I don't even know why I'm wearing this, I'm sure it's not necessary.'

'Well, I've no idea where it was you were sliced exactly but my guess is the doctors may be concerned that you suffered a trauma to the latissimus dorsi or your deltoid maybe.'

'Aye,' said Riley, none the wiser. 'That'll be it. So, what's happening with Ricci? Have you banged him up yet?'

'I'm not at liberty to say. You know that.'

'Aye, fair enough. It'd just be nice to know that the lunatic's behind bars, that's all.'

'Well, let's prove it was actually him who attacked you first, then we'll take it from there, okay?'

'Okay,' said Riley, 'but keep your eyes on him, Sergeant, we don't want him up to his old tricks again, not over here.'

'We'll do our best. So, what have you got for me?'

Riley opened the folder, pulled out a raft of papers, and slid them one by one across the desk.

'If I'm boring you with stuff you already know, just say so. These are copies of photos I managed to get off a fella called Matteo Bartolucci. He's a pathologist.'

'Pathologist?'

'Aye. He carried out the post-mortems on Ricci's victims in Siena.'

'Alleged victims.'

'Whatever.'

'So you just called him up and asked if he had some photos you could borrow?'

'Very good,' said Riley, 'but no. A few white lies and a fake email account. It's not difficult.'

'It's fraudulent,' said Dougal. 'And it's illegal.'

'It's what we call investigative journalism, Sergeant, without which half the crimes in this country would go unsolved. Besides, it's not as if it's hard evidence, it's just a few photos of a dead body.'

Dougal, hesitant at first, leafed through the first four prints and, in the absence of any obvious injuries, pushed them to one side.

'To be honest,' he said, 'she looks as though she passed away in her sleep, there's no…'

'No bruising?' said Riley. 'No sign of a struggle? That's why crap like this is manna from heaven for the likes of Ricci. Temazepam, MDMA, roofies, it's their get-out-of-jail-free card. See here, Sergeant, because the victim can't remember a damned thing, all the assailant has to do is insist that anything that occurred was consensual and nine times out of ten that's them away, off the hook, scot-free.'

'Right enough,' said Dougal. 'Look, I'm not sure how these photos can help us but I'll hang onto them all the same, if that's okay with you?'

'Aye, no bother. You keep them.'

'Is that it?'

'No, no,' said Riley. 'There's something else. Ricci, he's a wealthy man, right?'

'As far as I know.'

'Not just you, the whole of Tuscany. The press are always going on about how successful he is, what a philanthropist he is, how he likes to share his good fortune.'

'So?'

'So this is where things don't add up. I've been following his footsteps and I've pieced together a wee trail. It took a few weeks, I admit, but I've managed to figure out where he's been since he got here.'

'Have you aspirations to join the force?' said Dougal.

'You must be mad,' said Riley, 'and take orders from some fella with a few pips on his shoulders? No, no, I'm my own boss, that's not for me. Anyway, Alessandro Ricci, minted by all accounts, takes a Jet2 flight from Fiumicino to Glasgow. Why? Why a budget airline? Why not one of the major carriers? Why not first class?'

'I'll make a note to ask him next time I see him.'

'Not only that, if I were him I would've headed straight for the city centre and checked into the Hilton, or the Marriot, or the Argyll, but what does he do? He stops at the Travelodge on the outskirts of town.'

'You know what they say, Mr Riley, look after the pennies and the pounds will look after themselves.'

'I'm thinking pennies is all he's got. He's at the Travelodge for one night only, then he takes himself off to a B&B on Portland Road, which is one step up from a doss-house.'

'Considering what he's been through,' said Dougal, 'it's no surprise he wanted to keep his head down, especially if, as you mentioned in your article, an arrest warrant may be in the offing.'

'Then he's going about the wrong way. A couple of weeks later he did a flit. Legged it without settling his bill.'

'Did the owner not contact the police?'

'No chance. If he had, he'd have been hit with a string of fines for breach of health and safety.'

'So, where did he go after that? Got himself a wee flat somewhere nice, no doubt?'

'Not quite,' said Riley. 'He got himself a big house with all mod-cons and a live-in servant. He moved in with Helen Sullivan.'

'Doesn't hang around, does he? And is this where your trail ends?'

'For now,' said Riley, 'I'm still keeping tabs on him though, I want to see that nonce put away for good.'

Dougal, irritated yet intrigued by Riley's obsession with the émigré, pulled off his spectacles and polished them on his sweater.

'Don't take this the wrong way, Mr Riley,' he said, 'but your interest in Ricci seems to be bordering on fixation. Do you not think you're taking it all a bit too personally?'

'Aye, and rightly so. I mean, he shouldn't be allowed to get away with it, not after what he's done.'

'But why Ricci? How come you're not focusing on the home-grown druggies and dealers?'

'I have my reasons.'

'Anything to do with the free movement of criminals around the EU?'

'Maybe. And maybe not.'

'Look, you've saved me some work,' said Dougal, 'I'll give you that, but I think it's time you took a step back and let us handle this. I'm sure you'd not be happy if I had to charge you with obstruction or harassment now, would you?'

Riley, incensed at being belittled by someone who looked more like a university graduate on an internship than a fully-fledged police officer, refrained from unleashing a torrent of abuse and stood to leave.

'Wouldn't be the first time,' he said. 'I've dealt with your sort before.'

'What do you mean?' said Dougal.

'Doesn't matter. It's not important.'

'No, no. Go on. Are you saying you've been in trouble before?'

'Certainly not,' said Riley. 'It was wrongful arrest.'

'How so?'

'If you must know, I was covering a protest in Glasgow…'

'What kind of a protest?'

'What do you think? Independence.'

'When?'

'Years back.'

'And?'

'And nothing,' said Riley. 'It got out of hand and I was caught up in the melee.'

'Were you charged?'

'Don't be daft. They accused me of being party to an affray but they soon let me go.'

'As will I,' said Dougal just as West bounded through the door with Munro trailing in her wake. 'I'll be in touch.'

'Dougal!' said West. 'How's tricks?'

'Same as usual, miss. How was your trip?'

'Excellent. Arran was cool but the ride back from Ardrossan could've been better.'

'How so?'

'Jimbo, he's under the weather, bless him. Driving like a pensioner. Who's your mate?'

'This is Nick Riley,' said Dougal. 'Freelance journalist and amateur sleuth. He's just leaving.'

'Alright?' said West as she spied the sling. 'Oh hold up, you're the bloke who got whopped with a machete, right?'

'Aye, that's me.'

'You okay?'

'Never better.'

'Mr Riley was kind enough to give us some more info on Alessandro Ricci, miss.'

'Nice one. Every little helps.'

'I'm not so sure about that,' said Riley. 'Your sergeant here seems to think he has it all under control.'

Munro, feathers ruffled by Riley's sarcasm, crossed to the desk and shuffled through the pile of photos.

'Knowing Dougal,' he said like a protective patriarch defending his brood, 'he probably has. Where did these come from?'

'I brought them,' said Riley. 'That's one of the girls Ricci attacked in Siena.'

Munro winced as if suffering from a sudden bout of toothache and held one of the shots aloft.

'What do you know about this?' he said pointing to a detail of the girl's back.

'The tattoo?'

'It's hardly a tattoo. It's like she's been scratched with a penknife.'

'She probably was,' said Riley. 'Is it important?'

'Possibly. What does it mean?'

'It's the number seventeen, in Roman numerals.'

'And the significance is?'

Riley hesitated before glancing at Dougal with a smug smile smeared across his face and returned to his seat.

'In Italy,' he said, 'the number seventeen is like our thirteen. Some airlines don't have a seventeenth row, some buildings don't have a seventeenth floor, some...'

'I get the picture!' said Munro tersely. 'By jiminy, man, get to the point!'

'It's unlucky because the numerals can be rearranged to spell the word "vixi".

'Latin,' said Munro. 'I'm dead.'

'Correct. Otherwise translated as "I have lived" or "my life is over".'

'Thanking you, Mr Riley. You can leave now.'

'Leave? Are you joking me? But this was just getting interesting.'

Munro raised his head and fixed him with an ice-cold glare.

'Mr Riley. I said you can leave.'

West, perturbed by his ire, waited for the footsteps to fade along the corridor and turned to Munro.

'You're feeling better,' she said. 'What's up?'

'What's up, Charlie? I'll tell you what's up. Young Sophie Jackson has the self-same tattoo on her back. That's what's up. Dougal, have you any photos of Jessica Sullivan? Anything from McLeod?'

'I have,' said Dougal desperately trying to locate the folder on his desktop, 'here we go.'

With Munro and West hovering over his shoulders like a couple of vultures, he scrolled through a series of shots until Munro pointed excitedly at the screen and ordered him to stop.

'There!' he said. 'Jumping Jehoshaphat! Jessica has the same tattoo!'

'Surely that has to be enough to nail him,' said Dougal. 'Miss, what do you think?'

'If we can place him at the scene…'

'We can, aye.'

'Then I'd say you're right,' said West. 'Jimbo?'

'It's your call, lassie,' said Munro. 'In the meantime, I'll get a wee photo of Sophie's tattoo and send it to McLeod. Perhaps he can tell us how they were done.'

'Right. I think it's time we nipped downstairs and had a chat with this Ricci bloke. Anyone know the Italian for *you're going to need a lawyer*?'

'Not so fast, Charlie. One more thing. Dougal…'

'Boss?'

'…Ella MacCall.'

West drew a breath as Dougal stopped the flow of images cascading down the screen and zoomed in on a shot of MacCall's naked back.

'I don't believe it,' she said. 'It doesn't make sense. No tattoo.'

'There has to be a reason,' said Munro. 'If that's his calling card, then there has to be a reason.'

'I hope for all our sakes you're right,' said West, 'because if it wasn't Ricci who spiked her, then we're in trouble.'

Leaving Munro to cogitate in front of the screen with a mug of hot, sweet tea, West – skimming a crib-sheet penned in Dougal's immaculate hand-written script – headed for the interview room.

'Why do I get the feeling this is all going pear-shaped?'

'It's not, miss, not yet,' said Dougal. 'It's like the boss says, there has to be a reason and just now I'm thinking maybe it's because Ella MacCall wasn't just another victim, I mean, she and Ricci had a wee thing going, right? Maybe he thought of her as, I don't know, different?'

'Yeah, you might be right, Dougal. You might be right.'

Chapter 12

Alessandro Ricci, as cool as the proverbial cucumber, sat with his legs crossed and his arms folded, looking, despite a few hours in the cells, as immaculate as ever. He cocked his head and smiled as West took a seat at the desk opposite.

'Bellissima,' he said, his voice menacingly low.

'Mr Ricci. I'm Detective Inspector West and this is...'

'We've met.'

'Of course you have. Then you know why you're here.'

'A minor traffic violation. An oversight. It is easily resolved.'

'Under normal circumstances I'd agree with you,' said West as she scanned her notes, 'but as all your assets have been frozen and you have no access to your bank accounts, I really can't see how you're going to be able to stump up five grand.'

'It's not a problem,' said Ricci. 'Helen, Miss Sullivan, will take care of it.'

'Really? Is she that loaded?'

'She has enough.'

'Well I hope you're right. I wouldn't want to be in your shoes when the other inmates find out what you've been up to. Now then, before we try to *resolve* a few other issues, I understand you've waived your right to a solicitor, is that correct?'

'It is.'

'And you've not changed your mind?'

'No.'

'Good,' said West as she stabbed the voice-recorder, 'in that case I'd just like to remind you that you're still under caution. For the benefit of the tape I'm DI West, also present is DS McCrae and Mr Alessandro Ricci. The time is 4:22 pm. So, Mr Ricci, let's start with Ella MacCall. How did you meet?'

Ricci, looking mildly bemused, turned to Dougal and frowned.

'But I have already told the sergeant and his friend...'

'Friend?'

'The boss, miss.'

'...I have already told them, we have never met. It is still something I look forward to.'

West stood up, tucked her chair beneath the desk, and leaned against the wall.

'Let's not get off on the wrong foot,' she said, sighing as she checked her watch. 'I'm having a friend over for dinner and I don't want to be late. I have three witnesses who've seen you with MacCall on several occasions. In fact, they've even met you face to face.'

Ricci shook his head, smiled and raised his hands in defeat.

'Let me guess,' he said, 'Holly, Kirsty and Megan.'

'You've a memory for names.'

'Always. If a pretty girl is involved. Okay, Inspector, I lied and for that I apologise. I denied knowing her only to protect her. Some people find our age difference a little... strange.'

'Can't say I blame them,' said West. 'So, you admit to knowing her?'

'I do. She is a beautiful and talented young lady.'

'And when did you meet?'

'A few weeks ago.'

'Where?'

'The Irvine Community Sports Club. That is where she plays hockey.'

'Sorry,' said Dougal, 'but see here, Mr Ricci, I'm finding this just a wee bit creepy. Why would a fella your age be hanging around a ladies hockey club?'

'I went to visit them. They were looking for a sponsor. Someone who would pay for their kit.'

'And just how exactly did you know they were looking for funding?'

'An advertisement in the paper, the Kilmarnock Standard.'

'And you just happened to bump into Ella?' said West.

'I did,' said Ricci. 'She looked... lost. Upset. As though she needed someone to talk to.'

'So you thought you'd lend an ear?'

'And the rest,' said Dougal. 'When was the last time you saw her?'

'I have not seen her for at least a week. She was going on vacation.'

'To the Isle of Arran?'

'I think so.'

'Any idea how she got there?'

'I'm afraid not. One of her friends I imagine.'

'Aye,' said Dougal, 'it would be. Because you've never been, have you, Mr Ricci?'

'Let's try somebody else,' said West. 'Nick Riley.'

Ricci smiled at West and shrugged his shoulders.

'I have never heard of him,' he said. 'Nor have I ever met with him.'

'So you weren't wandering round Sandgate at...'

'Sorry. What is Sandgate?'

'It's a street,' said West, 'not far from here.'

'I know Kilmarnock, Inspector. I am not familiar with this area.'

'Okay. Strike three. Jessica Sullivan.'

'Ah, poor Jessica.'

'Aye, poor Jessica indeed,' said Dougal. 'Just how close were you and Jessica, Mr Ricci?'

'We were friends. Good friends. I think I was like an uncle to her.'

'Not a father?'

'That, I could never be.'

'So you went out together?' said West. 'Socially, I mean.'

'We did.'

'And you drank together?'

'Yes, and we went for supper together.'

'And did you sleep together?' said Dougal.

'It would be uncouth of me to answer such a question, Sergeant, demeaning as it is.'

'What about her mate?' said West. 'The girl you tried to pick up outside the nightclub. Sophie Jackson.'

'Is that her name? I didn't know.'

'Oh come off it, she visited Jessica at home several times. Are you telling me you never met?'

'No. I would have remembered, I am sure.'

'So, the first time you ever clapped eyes on her was outside the club?'

'That is correct,' said Ricci. 'When Jessica telephoned to ask if I would pick her up from the club, she simply said her friend needed a ride home too.'

'But she didn't go with you?'

'No. She decided to make her own way home.'

'Well, she nearly didn't make it.'

'I cannot be blamed for that,' said Ricci. 'Young people in this country, Inspector, they do not know how to drink, only how to get drunk.'

'And was Jessica drunk?'

'A little, I think.'

'So, despite the fact that she'd had a few, you still didn't think to see her home safely?'

'She insisted. And if there's one thing I know how to do well, it is to respect a lady's wishes.'

'God preserve us,' said West. 'Helen Sullivan. How's your relationship with Helen Sullivan?'

'It has its ups. And it has its downs.'

'So you're not thinking of trading her in for a younger model?'

'Please, show some decorum, Inspector. You're letting yourself down.'

Believing Ricci to be a misogynistic, pompous ass with psychotic tendencies who suffered from delusions of grandeur, West – making a mental note to earmark him for a psychiatric assessment – slid her hands into her pockets and walked slowly towards the rear of the room.

'How are you getting by at the moment, Mr Ricci?' she said. 'I mean, how do you pay for stuff? Rent, food, petrol?'

'Cash,' said Ricci without turning his head. 'I pay in cash.'

'You brought it with you?'

'I did.'

'That's not going to last long, is it? The legal limit without declaring it is ten grand. Any more than that and that's another fine you're in for. How much did you bring?'

'I'd rather not say.'

'Dear, dear,' said West as she returned to the desk, 'that's an admission of guilt if ever I heard one. Tell me, Mr Ricci, are you superstitious at all?'

'Superstition is for those who cannot control their own destiny.'

'So, you wouldn't think the number seventeen unlucky?'

'No.'

'And how's your Latin?'

'Excellent.'

'Vixi?'

128

'Come, come,' said Ricci. 'You're young, Inspector. You've your whole life ahead of you, I'm sure.'

* * *

Though blessed with the spindly physique of a long-distance runner, Dougal – who possessed the athletic prowess of a pot-bellied pig in a paddy field – struggled to match West as she scurried up the four flights of stairs.

'Are you okay, miss?' he said, trying to catch his breath, 'you're in an awful hurry.'

'There's something I need to do.'

'But hold on, are we not charging him?'

'What?'

'Ricci, are we not charging him?'

'No, not yet. So far as MacCall's concerned, we need to prove he was on that ferry.'

'Right enough,' said Dougal, 'but we can't hold him much longer, time's running out.'

'Tell me about it,' said West, 'if push comes to shove, we'll do him for the insurance first, that'll buy us some time. Oh, and before I forget, I need you to ring Mackenzie in Brodick and find out when McIver's coming over...'

'No bother,' said Dougal.

'...and when you've done that, call the hockey club and see if they can verify Ricci's story. I want to know if he really was interested in sponsoring them or just hanging around the playground.'

* * *

Munro, confounded by the image of MacCall's unblemished torso, was still staring at the screen when West, clearly agitated, barged through the door.

'Ah, you're back,' he said. 'And how's Casanova? Did you not get a signed confession?'

'No,' said West. 'All I got was a touch of the collywobbles. I think I need a shower just from being in the same room as him.'

'That's not the reason you're in a strop, Charlie. What's up?'

'You'll see,' said West, 'just give me a minute. Dougal, the CCTV from Sandgate...'

'Miss.'

'...I haven't seen it yet, run it for me, would you?'

Munro sat back and smiled with anticipation as West watched the film unfold.

'Jimbo,' she said. 'Have you seen this?'

'I have indeed.'

'And?'

'You tell me.'

'It's not him, is it?' said West. 'The bloke with the machete, it's not Ricci.'

'Are you joking me?' said Dougal. 'How can you tell? He's covered from head to toe.'

'Oh come on, Dougal, do you need a trip to Specsavers or what? Ricci's built like a twig and he's got to be at least five-eleven if not six feet. Riley's a short arse, he's what? Five-six, five-seven? The geezer attacking him's about the same height. And he's stocky. He's too short and he's too stocky to be Ricci.'

'Jeez-oh,' said Dougal, 'Why did I not get that?'

'You're run down, laddie,' said Munro. 'You need a break.'

'Aye, maybe so.'

'There's no maybe about it.'

'Jimbo,' said West, 'if you knew that wasn't Ricci, then why didn't you say so?'

'It's not my place,' said Munro. 'And it's not my job anymore. Besides I knew you'd get there soon enough. Why the frown?'

'I just had a thought. If Ricci was wound up because he got wind of Riley's article then that would have made sense, right? But if it wasn't him waving the blade about, and if it wasn't a random attack, then who the hell was it?'

'Och, you know what journalists are like, lassie, it's probably someone with a grudge.'

'Then why is Riley so flipping adamant that it was Ricci?'

'I asked him the same question, miss,' said Dougal. 'It's like the man's obsessed.'

'I don't know about obsessed, but he's got an attitude alright. So, what do we do now?'

Munro, feeling unusually warm, loosened his tie and rang a finger around his collar.

'Instinct lassie,' he said. 'Use your instinct.'

'You and your flipping instinct,' said West, 'you're beginning to sound like Obi-Wan Kenobi: *feel the force, Luke, feel the force.*'

'I'm glad you find it amusing but if it wasnae for my instinct you'd not be here.'

'Really?'

'Aye. I'll not mince my words, Charlie. I'll have you remember that when we met you were struggling, struggling with your career and blaming your own inadequacies for a failed relationship and you thought the answer lay in the bottom of a bottle of booze. You may have been a wreck, lassie, but my instinct told me you had the potential to be one of the best. And look at you now.'

West, in a moment of quiet contemplation, turned her back on Munro, reached for the kettle and, realising that the sun had long set over the yardarm, decided that the time for coffee had passed and a large Balvenie was on the cards.

'Dougal,' she said, as she smiled apologetically at Munro, 'instinct tells me we should run a quick check on Riley…'

'On it, miss.'

'…see if he's got any previous and find out if he's ever been to Tuscany, maybe he and Ricci have got a history.'

'There you go,' said Munro grinning. 'Sometimes, Charlie, all you need is a size twelve up the backside.'

'Sometimes, Jimbo, a gentle nudge would do.'

'Miss!' said Dougal excitedly, 'forgive me for saying so, but my instinct tells me you're not going to like this.'

'Don't tell me, he's got form.'

'I wouldn't know, I'm only on the electoral register.'

'And?'

'Riley, he lives alone. He's got a one bedroom flat right here on Bath Place, not far from the beach.'

'So, what's the big deal?'

'Up until last year there were two people registered at that address. The other was Helen Sullivan.'

Chapter 13

Despite a drop in temperature sharp enough to freeze the fur off an Arctic fox, Munro – warmed by a large single malt – stood in his shirt sleeves on the balcony of West's first floor apartment on North Harbour Street and, gazing across the Firth beneath a star-studded sky, mulled over his options concerning the deferral of his own demise.

Regarding the notion of a six hour operation, during which the surgeons would pillage the veins from his legs before breaking open his breastbone to graft them onto his heart as a fanciful non-starter, he dallied instead with the concept of relying on beta-blockers and statins to alleviate his symptoms, before concluding that they amounted to nothing more than a sticking-plaster on what was essentially a dire prognosis.

Raising his glass to the heavens, he dismissed his only other alternative – a life devoid of dairy, bacon butties, and slices of raw-aged Aberdeen Angus pan-fried in beef dripping – as needlessly masochistic and resigned himself to his fate, smiling as West, clutching the bottle of Balvenie, joined him outside.

'Are you mad?' she said, quivering against the cold, 'you'll catch your death.'

'Too late for that, lassie.'

'What? You're bonkers, you are. Look, if you're in a huff because of earlier then I'm sorry, okay? I didn't mean to snap, things are just a bit fraught, that's all.'

'I'm not in a huff, Charlie, and there's no need to apologise, you know that.'

'Good,' said West as she topped up his glass. 'I don't know what you're so flipping miserable about but if you ask me, Dougal's not the only one who could do with a break.'

'I'm not in need of a break.'

'You bleeding well are,' said West, 'you just don't know it. Face facts, Jimbo, you're cream-crackered. You almost killed yourself when your gaff blew up, then you legged it off to Skye, you've been living out of a suitcase for God knows how long, and to cap it all when you're not trying to decorate your house, you've got the emotional stress of finding your mate's daughter drugged-up to the eyeballs to deal with. Trust me, you need a holiday before you keel over.'

'I'll let you into a secret,' said Munro, 'me and holidays were separated at birth.'

'Well it's time you had a reunion. I'm going to book you something if it's the last thing I do.'

* * *

Not one to renege on a deal, Munro – keeping to his side of the bargain – opened a bottle of Bordeaux, filled two tumblers to the brim, and sat poised at the table while West, ignoring the buzz of her phone, seared the steaks and pulled the chips from under the grill.

'Are you not getting that?'

'One pair of hands, Jimbo. Whoever it is will have to wait. Patience, as they say, is a virtue.'

'Right enough,' said Munro, 'but it's not one of mine.'

Relenting, West took a swig of wine, yanked her phone from her hip, and rolled her eyes.

* * *

Though no stranger to the bitter conditions of a winter in the Lowlands, Duncan – driving with his mobile wedged firmly between his ear and the hem of his woolly watch cap – shuddered as the biting breeze blasting through the vents of the decrepit Defender cut him to the core.

'Duncan,' said West, 'can I call you back?'

'No chance, miss. It's pure Baltic here, I need to get this conversation over with.'

'But we're just about to eat.'

'Good for you,' said Duncan, 'I've had to make do with a cheeseburger and a milkshake.'

'Where are you?'

'I'm heading back to the office. I'm going to leave your motor in the pound…'

'Crikey, I forgot about that.'

'…and with any luck it'll get towed away.'

'Thanks, mate. Anything else?'

'Aye. Happy Christmas.'

'You what?'

'Result, miss. On the flask.'

'No way!' said West. 'Right, hold on, I'm going to stick you on speaker but you'll have to yell. Okay, what did they find?'

'Tomato soup.'

'No time for jokes, Duncan, I'm dishing up.'

'It's no joke. The flask contained tomato soup and the cup had two lovely samples of DNA.'

'Two?'

'Aye. One's a positive for Ella MacCall but there's no match for the other.'

'No match?' said West. 'No, no. That can't be right, I mean it has to be Ricci. It just has to be.'

'It probably is,' said Munro, 'but it's too soon, Charlie. His profile will not be on the system yet.'

'Is that you, chief?' said Duncan. 'Are you okay?'

'Surviving laddie. I'm surviving.'

'Glad to hear it. The chief's right, miss. I'd not panic, not just yet.'

'Well if it's not there tomorrow,' said West, 'you'll have to get FS to do it, got that? Right, get yourself home and…'

'I'm not finished yet.'

'What now?'

'The girls.'

'Of course,' said West. 'Sorry, mate. How'd you get on?'

'Good and bad,' said Duncan. 'I spoke to Megan Dalgleish and Holly Paterson first. They know something, I can tell, but they're not saying. They just clammed up. Didn't help having their parents in the same room but we could bring them in, I mean they're not juveniles anymore.'

'Maybe,' said West. 'I hope that's the bad?'

'Oh aye. Now for the good: Kirsty Young. She said there is something she wants to tell us but she's too scared. She'll not say a thing unless we can guarantee her safety.'

'She wants protection?'

'Aye, miss. She's afraid of reprisals.'

'From who? Ricci?'

'I've no idea. Will I tell her yes?'

West, biting her bottom lip, pondered as she piled the French fries onto the plates.

'Okay look,' she said. 'Dougal's already charged Ricci on the insurance ticket which means even if he doesn't go down, he'll be out of harm's way for a couple of days at least so yeah, do it. You can pick her up in the morning.'

'Roger that, miss. And if it's not Ricci she's worried about?'

'We'll cross that bridge when we come to it.'

Baffled by his insouciance, West hung up, sat down, and eyed Munro with a hint of suspicion.

'Well,' she said. 'Aren't you going to ask?'

'Ask what, Charlie?'

'About MacCall, the DNA on the flask. Kirsty Young wanting to spill the beans?'

'No, no,' said Munro. 'If it's all the same with you, lassie, I'd rather get acquainted with my supper.'

'That's not like you, Jimbo. That's not like you at all.'

* * *

As an authority on the foibles of human nature, Munro had rightly attributed the stabilising influence of a steady girlfriend as the reason behind Duncan's new-found fervour for the cerebral side of policing. Dougal, however, remained unimpressed with his significant other's inability to quash his predilection for dressing like a jakey and his aversion to the benefits of a boil-wash.

'Jeez-oh!' he said as he bounced through the door, 'it's not even seven, did you not sleep?'

'I'll have you know I was up with the birds. A look like this doesn't come easy.'

'I'll take your word for it,' said Dougal, 'but why so early?'

'I've an errand to run.'

'The launderette?'

'Aye, that's funny, pal. It's Kilmarnock actually. I'm to fetch Kirsty Young. She's a tale to tell and if I'm right it involves a fella by the name of Ricci and a wee ride on a ferry.'

'That's smashing,' said Dougal. 'If she can place him behind the wheel then we can hang him out to dry.'

'Exactly. So I'll have myself a wee brew then that's me away. How about you?'

'Nick Riley. I'm going to scoot over to his place and find out if there was anything going on between him and Helen Sullivan or if she was just renting a room.'

'My money's on a room with benefits,' said Duncan. 'Is Westie not here yet?'

'Westie,' said West as she tossed her jacket on the desk, 'is right behind you.'

'Sorry, miss. I didn't mean to…'

'Relax.'

'Is the chief not with you?'

'Nope. He mumbled something about turpentine and took off like a shot. Truth be known, I think he's run-down, big-style. Dougal, you know him as well as anyone, where do you think he'd go if he wanted a holiday?'

'No-brainer, miss,' said Dougal. 'Islay. Do you not remember that's where he and wife went on their honeymoon?'

'Of course it was. Okay, one of you two do me a favour, see if you can get him a decent hotel for a week or two, or better still, a cottage.'

'No bother,' said Duncan, 'I'll take a look now before I head off. Is this to go on expenses?'

'No,' said West. 'My treat. Let's call it an early birthday present. Right, let's crack on. Dougal, give me some good news while you stick the kettle on.'

'Sorry, miss, no can do.'

'Why? Are we out of milk?'

'Plenty of milk. Just a shortage of good news. Brace yourself.'

'I'm listening.'

'I spoke to Mackenzie. He doesn't have a scooby where he is.'

'You what?'

'McIver. He's not home and the garage is all locked up.'

West, momentarily stunned by the revelation that her number two suspect could be hundreds of miles away, looked to the ceiling and cursed.

'Dammit!' she said, slamming the table. 'That's all we need. When was he last seen?'

'The pub last night,' said Dougal. 'He popped in about six o'clock but he didn't hang about.'

'And it's taken this long to find out he's legged it?'

'In all fairness, miss, they probably assumed he'd just gone home. Mackenzie says he only became concerned when the garage didn't open for business this morning.'

'Okay,' said West. 'Get him on the blower, tell him to scour the whole island, maybe his mountain rescue mates know where he is. Our friend McIver's just pipped Ricci to the top spot. Hold up, what time's the first ferry from Brodick to Ardrossan?'

'Eight-twenty, miss. I've already checked.'

'So he's still got plenty of time to make that. Make sure Mackenzie has someone down there just in case, then call CalMac and get a passenger list for all the sailings since six o'clock last night.'

'On it,' said Dougal as he handed her a brew. 'I do have some other news, it's not brilliant but at least it proves Ricci's not a habitual liar.'

'What's that?'

'The hockey club. He did go to see them after all. He met with the manager, a Miss Sarah Crawford, but she's not happy with him.'

'Why not?'

'He was that keen she thought they had a deal but she's not heard from him since. It's a shame really because they're really quite good, they came fourth in the national league last year.'

'I didn't know you were into hockey,' said Duncan. 'Is that what floats your boat, all those short skirts and big, navy blue knickers?'

'That's enough,' said West. 'Besides, that's netball.'

'See here, miss,' said Dougal as he spun his laptop round, 'this is the most recent photo on their website. That's young Ella MacCall on the end there and by the looks of it, she's not too happy about losing.'

West, reminded of her school days and her absolute hatred of anything sporty, scrutinised the image and, unsettled by what she saw, called across the room.

'Duncan,' she said, clicking her fingers. 'Here. Quick.'

'Do I have to, miss?' he said as he ambled over, 'it's not really my…'

'Remind you of anyone?'

Duncan placed his hands on the desk, leaned forward and groaned in disbelief as his eyes focused on the lissom blonde standing behind Ella MacCall.

'Is that not McIver's pal?' he said. 'The PE teacher?'

'If it isn't,' said West as she sipped her tea, 'then she's got a double. You'd better get yourself some Kwells, you might need them.'

Chapter 14

With Duncan and Dougal on their respective assignments and Munro busy scouring the shelves of the local hardware store for a bottle of paint thinners, West – relishing the unique experience of being alone in the office – seized the opportunity to take a peek at the two cottages Duncan had left bookmarked on the screen and, though pleasantly surprised by his choices, dismissed the first on the grounds that she wasn't a millionaire whilst the owners, judging by the price of a week's rental, probably were.

The second, however – a traditional, white-washed crofter's cottage in Port Ellen - was set on a private beach not far from the Carraig Fhada lighthouse and, apart from being affordable, enjoyed a commanding view across the North Channel to Rathlin Island and regular visits from schools of Bottlenose dolphins and hungry sea otters.

Questioning the validity of the old adage '*it is better to give than it is to receive*' she tapped in her credit card details and finalised the booking before turning her attention to the job in hand.

* * *

'PC Mackenzie,' West said. 'How's it going?'

'Aye, all good, Inspector. And yourself?'

'Could be better. Any luck with McIver?'

'Not yet,' said Mackenzie. 'I'm still waiting on CalMac for the passenger list. I've done the rounds again and he's not been seen since last night.'

'Is he in the habit of taking off like this? Doing a disappearing act out of the blue?'

'No, no. That's what worries me. See here, Inspector, even if John was just hopping across to the mainland, he'd always tell someone where he was going.'

'And he's not doing anything with mountain rescue, like a training exercise or something?'

'No. I've checked. They've nothing scheduled and they've not had a call-out.'

'Well, keep looking,' said West. 'You never know, he might have had an accident.'

'Aye, right enough. Rest assured we'll keep our eyes open.'

'Okay listen, I need to have a word with his mate, Isla Thomson.'

'Oh, no need,' said Mackenzie. 'I already told your Sergeant McCrae, she's not seen him either.'

'It's not McIver I need to speak to her about. Have you got a number?'

'I have indeed but she's probably busy just now, preparing for lessons. Will I not just ask her to give you a call?'

'No thanks,' said West. 'Number please.'

'As you wish, Inspector. As you wish.'

* * *

Assuming that she owned a car without the benefits of Bluetooth or was simply in the habit of not taking unsolicited calls, West – refusing to leave a voicemail – repeatedly hung up and redialled until a less-than-cheerful Thomson finally answered her phone.

'Who the hell is this?' she said curtly, 'I'm trying to get to…'

'Isla Thomson? It's DI West. We met at McIver's garage.'

'Could you not just leave a message?'

'People have a habit of ignoring messages,' said West. 'And this is important.'

'Well if it's John you're after, then for the umpteenth time, I've not seen him.'

'Aren't you worried about him? I mean, he's your mate, you work together?'

'He's a grown man,' said Thomson, 'he can look after himself.'

'Charming,' said West. 'Anyway, this is nothing to do with McIver.'

'What then?'

'I'm calling about the Irvine Community Sports Club.'

'What of it?'

'You never said you coached a hockey team there.'

'Why should I? It's not important, is it?'

'It is when Ella MacCall was on your team.'

West sat back and smiled at the ensuing silence.

'I see,' said Thomson, sheepishly.

'Why didn't you tell us you knew her?'

'You never asked.'

'Okay,' said West, 'then why didn't you tell McIver when you found her on Goat Fell? Or PC Mackenzie? Or the ambulance crew?'

'Because it wasn't worth it,' said Thomson. 'Look inspector, I hardly knew the girl, she was just another player on the team. Besides, if you'd seen what she looked like when we found her, even I couldn't be sure it was her.'

'Fair enough, but even if you had your doubts you should've said something to Mackenzie. At the very least it would've saved us a lot of time and trouble.'

'Sorry I couldn't make your life easier,' said Thomson. 'Is that it?'

'Not quite,' said West. 'I understand your club was looking for a new sponsor…'

'Hold on. A sponsor? What's that got to do with anything?'

'As I was saying,' said West, 'you were looking for a new sponsor. Have you found anyone yet?'

'I'm not sure. You'll have to speak with Sarah Crawford. The last I heard she was doing a deal with Alex.'

'Alex? You mean Alessandro Ricci?'

'Aye, that's him.'

'Why do you call him Alex?'

'Because that's how he introduced himself.'

'So you've met?'

'Aye, a few times. Nice fella.'

'So, you know him quite well?' said West. 'Mr Ricci?'

'Not inside-out but well enough.'

'In what way? I mean, do you socialise together?'

'That's none of your business.'

'Sounds like an admission of guilt to me,' said West. 'You do know he's got a partner, don't you?'

For the second time in what was turning out to be a revealing conversation, West smiled and waited patiently for a response.

'No,' said Thomson. 'I did not.'

'He's quite the player, your mate Alex, wouldn't you say? What did Ella think of him?'

'Ella?'

'That's right. I'm assuming you know that she and he were…'

'Are you joking me?' said Thomson. 'No, that's not right, he's old enough to be her…'

'I'm deadly serious, Miss Thomson.'

'Well, if it's true then I'll not be seeing him again. There ought to be a law against that kind of thing.'

'There is,' said West, 'in a manner of speaking.'

'Well, if you're done, I've a class to teach.'

'Then I won't keep you,' said West. 'Oh, and a word to the wise, Miss Thomson, don't go doing a disappearing act like your mate McIver. I might be coming to see you soon.'

'Is that a threat, Inspector?'

'No. Just a friendly invitation to stick the kettle on.'

* * *

Regarding Thomson's association with Ricci to be, at best, an ill-judged dalliance, and her cold-hearted indifference to MacCall's demise the result of ferrying countless cadavers down the mountainside, West remained, nonetheless, intrigued as to why Ella MacCall was the only one in the team photograph to look so desperately unhappy.

Staring intently at the photo on Dougal's laptop, she sought clues in her defensive stance, her aversion to the camera, and her dour expression until, becoming increasingly frustrated, she closed the window to focus her attention on Ricci's two other victims.

Mindful of the fact that she'd need irrefutable proof that the tattooed inscriptions on the backs of Sullivan and Jackson were born of the same hand and not two different members of some burgeoning cult, she placed the magnified images side by side and scrutinised their wounds before calling McLeod for some much-needed reassurance.

'Charlotte. This is a pleasant surprise.'

'Alright, Andy? How the devil are you?

'Oh, same as usual,' said McLeod. 'Up to my wotsits in death and decay, rotting flesh and dismembered limbs.'

'I'm beginning to realise why I've never dated a pathologist. Speaking of which, have you had a close encounter with a razor yet?'

'Why? Do you fear the beard?'

'I fear what's living in it.'

'Well, in answer to your question,' said McLeod, 'the answer is no.'

'Shame. Better keep this strictly business then. Did you get a photo of Jessica Sullivan's mate, the girl with a similar tattoo?'

'Sophie Jackson? I did, aye. She's lucky not to have ended up on my slab as well.'

'You're not wrong there,' said West. 'Okay, look, I need to be absolutely sure both tattoos were the work of the same person and I've had some thoughts.'

'On you go.'

'Well, I'm no expert but it looks to me as if the same implement was used in both cases, nothing as sharp as a scalpel, but nothing too dull either. Obviously a blade of sorts, but probably one that's been used.'

'Very good,' said McLeod. 'And what makes you think that?'

'The cuts,' said West, 'they're not clean. They're more like scratches, it's as if the skin's been, what's the word, tugged? Like it snagged on the blade.'

'Anything else?'

'Yeah, I'm not sure about this but in both cases the letter 'I' seems to bend slightly at the base so I'm thinking the perp was right-handed.'

'So, what do you need from me?'

'Some reassurance. Am I right or am I off the mark?'

'Put it this way,' said McLeod, 'should you ever feel the urge to walk with the dead, you'd sail through medical school. You're on the money, Charlotte. Full marks.'

'Cheers, Andy. Appreciate it.'

'Now if you could just find the tool that he used to carve those initials, you'd be home dry.'

'Any ideas?'

'Well the incisions aren't deep,' said McLeod, 'so something small. And rather than a dull blade, perhaps it's one that wasn't designed to be too sharp.'

'That doesn't make sense,' said West.

'It makes perfect sense. You've an image in your head of a flat piece of metal with a sharp point. Perhaps you should be thinking of a cutlery knife, maybe one with a serrated edge, or one of those blades you get attached to a corkscrew.'

'Genius!' said West. 'As it happens, the bloke I've got my eye on owns a vineyard. Maybe he carries one around with him?'

'It's not unheard of.'

'You're a diamond. Right, I'm not being rude but I have to get on, I need to call my sergeant.'

'Listen, before you go, I don't suppose…'

'One word, Andy: Bic.'

* * *

As someone who spent most of the night glued to his computer screen, tablet, or iPhone, Dougal – an earnest enigmatologist driven by the multitude of unorthodox cases which landed on his desk – was on the whole content with his largely windowless apartment until he clapped eyes on Riley's sprawling, light-filled flat overlooking the esplanade at the end of Bath Place and he suddenly realised, not without a hint of jealousy, that his gloomy pad had more in common with The Black Hole of Calcutta than the bijou homage to modern living the estate agent had enthused about.

'If it's not a good time,' he said as he removed his crash helmet, 'I can always come back later.'

'No, you're alright,' said Riley. 'Come on through to the lounge, I'm just having myself some breakfast. Can I get you a coffee?'

'Aye, go on.'

Dougal pulled up a chair and made a cursory glance of the room while he waited for Riley to return. An antique oak filing cabinet from the glory days of journalism sat in the corner, a television set with the sound turned down was tuned to CNN, and a handful of framed photos were scattered higgledy-piggledy across the wall but most interesting of all was the pile of newspapers stacked behind the door.

'Milk, one sugar,' said Riley as he handed him a mug. 'I forgot to ask so I guessed.'

'Spot on,' said Dougal, 'cheers. Tell me, Mr Riley, I'm curious, what's with all the newspapers? I mean, is that not a wee bit odd, particularly for someone in your profession?'

'Maybe. The fact is, I find them easier on the eye than a blessed computer. My sight's not great at the best of times.'

'Aye, I get what you're saying. The funny thing is, technology's meant to make our lives easier but in reality, it's making us all blind.'

'God, you're a cheery soul,' said Riley. 'So, what's up? I take it you're not here to brush up on your Latin?'

'Sorry?'

'Vixi.'

'Oh aye,' said Dougal, 'no. It's not that.'

'What then?'

'Have you lived here long?'

Riley, taken aback by a question that was clearly irrelevant as far as the investigation was concerned, frowned inquisitively and joined him at the table.

'Long enough,' he said.

'And have you always lived alone?'

'I have.'

'You're quite sure?' said Dougal. 'I mean, you've never taken a lodger for example? Or maybe rented a room to a student?'

'Not with one bedroom, no. Where exactly are you going with this?'

'Round in circles by the looks of it. See here, Mr Riley, I ran a check against the electoral register and it states quite clearly that somebody else used to live here too. At the same time as you. A Miss Helen Sullivan.'

'I see,' said Riley, shifting in his seat.

'And what I can't get my head around is why you didn't mention it, especially as she's now living with Alessandro Ricci. But with all the research you've done, I'm sure you knew that anyway.'

'I did,' said Riley, nodding. 'I've known for a while.'

'So?'

'We're history, Sergeant. We had a thing once but it didn't work out, so we parted company. End of story.'

'As simple as that?'

'Life doesn't have to be complicated.'

Dougal, staring blankly into space, paused to sip his coffee as he quietly contemplated his next question.

'Tell me if I'm being nosey, Mr Riley,' he said, 'but do you still have feelings for Miss Sullivan? I mean, is that why you have it in for Ricci? Because you're jealous?'

'I'm not jealous!' said Riley with an unconvincing laugh. 'She's moved on and so have I. We're free agents.'

'So, you're not waging some kind of a vendetta against him?'

'Oh, I am. But as a journalist, Sergeant, not a malevolent ex. You have a copy of my article, you should check the date. You'll see I started writing it just days after Ricci landed in Glasgow, long before he shacked up with Helen. Now, if that's everything, I have some work to...'

'Not quite,' said Dougal as he gestured for Riley to return to his seat. 'I realise you're a busy man but there's something else I need to ask you about.'

'Well, make it quick.'

'The fella who attacked you. You claim it was Ricci.'

'One hundred percent positive.'

'Even though he came at you from behind?'

'Okay, ninety-five percent positive.'

'And he was running away by the time you realised you'd been hit?'

'Let's say ninety and call it quits.'

'So, you're not changing your mind?' said Dougal. 'Even though not ten minutes ago you admitted to me that your eyesight's not that great?'

Looking as nervous as the hunter who'd become the hunted, Riley, uneasy about the probing, personal questions, brushed imaginary crumbs from the table as Dougal finished his coffee.

'The thing is, Mr Riley, we've got your attack on CCTV. Now, I'd say you're about five feet seven. Am I right?'

'Five seven and a half. Why?'

'Alessandro Ricci,' said Dougal as he made for the door, 'he's a good six feet. But you know that, don't you? I'll be in touch.'

* * *

Irritated by his own inability to instantly establish a motive for Riley's dogged pursuit of Ricci, Dougal – straddling his scooter with his helmet hanging from the handlebars – gazed across the deserted beach and reached for his phone.

'Alright, miss?' he said. 'You okay?'

'Yeah, are you on your way back?'

'Aye, all done. My head's mince.'

'How d'you mean?'

'Riley,' said Dougal. 'He's admitted to having a relationship with Helen Sullivan and he knows that's she's living with Ricci, okay? But I'm not convinced that's a good enough reason to persecute the fella. I mean, I know he come across as bitter and twisted, but jealous? I think there has to be more to this, surely.'

'So he's still claiming it was Ricci who attacked him?'

'He is, aye. But we know, and he knows, it wasn't.'

'In that case,' said West, 'it sounds to me as if he's trying to protect his attacker. Like he knows who it is but he's trying to pin it on Ricci.'

'But surely if he didn't want his attacker to get caught it'd be a lot easier if he just said nothing? Why go after Ricci?'

'To be honest,' said West, 'I really don't know and quite frankly some second-rate journalist getting a scratch on the arm is the least of my worries. Now listen up: that Insignia…'

'Miss?'

'Did SOCOs find anything unusual on board? Like a penknife or a corkscrew?'

'A corkscrew?'

'Yeah, I've been talking to McLeod and he reckons…'

'We should be looking for a boy scout or a wine merchant?'

'Very funny.'

'Nothing like that, miss.'

'What about Ricci's personal effects? Was he carrying anything like that when you checked him in?'

'No, just some jewellery,' said Dougal. 'All his gear and the stuff from the car is all bagged up in the usual place if you want it.'

'Good,' said West. 'Now get your arse back as quick as you can. We might need to organise a search of Sullivan's gaff. If we don't find whatever it was he used to cut the girls, then we're going to lose him.'

'On my way.'

'Incidentally, I don't suppose you've heard from Jimbo, have you?'

'No, miss. Why?'

'He was only popping down the DIY store and he's been gone ages, I thought he'd have been back by now.'

'Oh, I wouldn't fret, miss, you know the boss. He's probably foraging through the gardening section looking for spring bulbs.'

Chapter 15

Having consumed nothing more than the usual bowl of porridge, two fried eggs, bacon, toast, and a grilled tomato, Munro – bewildered by the onset of yet another bout of burning dyspepsia – popped a peppermint into his mouth and, blaming West's culinary skills for what might eventually be diagnosed as a debilitating case of salmonella, rang the bell and stood back.

Looking as weary as a pit pony after a gruelling eight-hour shift, Sullivan – still in her nightwear – opened the door, wiped the sleep from her eyes, and greeted Munro with a jaded smile.

'What are you now?' she said, fumbling through her pocket for a cigarette. 'A door to door salesman?'

'You've lost me,' said Munro.

'The turpentine.'

Munro smiled and slipped the bottle into his pocket.

'The ironmongers,' he said. 'It's the only place I could find it. Would you mind if we had a wee chat, Miss Sullivan?'

'Is this official business?'

'As I am no longer a serving member of Police Scotland, I would have to say the answer is no.'

'Then you'd best come in.'

Disheartened by the growing pile of crusty crockery, mouldy pizza boxes and assorted takeaway wrappers still languishing on the bookcase, Munro – his nose twitching against the lingering aroma of a half-eaten chicken tikka masala – grimaced as Sullivan pulled her dressing gown tight around her waist and sat down.

'Are you okay?' she said as she lit her cigarette. 'Can I get you a tea or something.'

'No, no,' said Munro. 'Very kind but dinnae trouble yourself. It's just a touch of indigestion.'

'A wee glass of milk then?'

'Really, I'm fine. It'll pass.'

'Well, if you're sure. So, *unofficially*, why are you here, Mr Munro? Is this about Jessica?'

'Not directly. No.'

'Alex then? Is he still banged up?'

'He is,' said Munro, 'but I'm afraid I cannae say much more than that.'

'I understand.'

'It's not because I dinnae want to, it's because I've no idea how the case is progressing. You'll have to speak with DS McCrae, he'll know when he's due in court.'

'Do you think he'll go down?'

'Well, unless you've a few grand hidden about the place…'

Sullivan smiled and stubbed out her cigarette.

'I'll take that as a yes, then.'

'You seem pleased.'

'More relieved than pleased.'

'So, the honeymoon's over and now you're saddled with reality, is that it?'

'It's more than that.'

'I'll not pry, Miss Sullivan, but if there's something you want to tell me, well that's entirely up to you.'

'Aye, okay,' said Sullivan. 'I'll tell you something. He played me like a fiddle and I fell for it hook, line and sinker.'

'How so?'

'The charm,' said Sullivan. 'The sophistication. I was a fool, punching above my weight. I mean, what the hell was I thinking? A toff, an Italian toff at that, falling for the likes of me? I must need my head testing.'

'Dinnae put yourself down, Miss Sullivan. You're better than that.'

'Maybe. Don't get me wrong, things were great to start with, you know, nice and cosy. The restaurants, the flowers, he'd even surprise me with a wee present every now and then.'

'So, what happened?'

'The money ran out is what happened. He saved himself a few quid by moving in with me, that's for sure, but as I say, that's when things turned sour. When his money ran out.'

'You mean he was borrowing from you?'

'Aye, not much,' said Sullivan. 'A few quid here and there, but it's not the money that bothered me, Mr Munro. It was the fact that he hardly went out. That he was here all the time. Alone. With Jessica.'

'I see. Forgive me for asking, Miss Sullivan, I dinnae want to seem insensitive, but do you think he and your daughter were…'

'I hope not, for all our sakes, because if they have…'

'Then what, Miss Sullivan?'

'Nothing. Look I don't know what they got up to but there was a point when Jessica just went weird on me, it's like she'd started to resent me. She'd not come home until the wee hours, she'd not speak, she just avoided me like the…'

Sullivan paused, grabbed the sleeve of her gown, and wiped her eyes.

'Here,' said Munro as he handed her a crisp, white handkerchief. 'You're not as hard as you make out, are you, Miss Sullivan?'

'I'm not hard at all, Mr Munro. A marshmallow on legs, that's me. See here, I loved my daughter, I loved her with every beat of my heart and I miss her every single second of the day.'

'Well you cannae blame yourself for what happened.'

'I don't. I blame Alex.'

'Did you ever confront him about his... behaviour?'

'I did, aye.'

'And?'

'I was told in no uncertain terms to mind my own business.'

'From where I'm standing, Miss Sullivan, I'd say Jessica was your business.'

'Right enough, but he said if I didn't keep my nose out, then he'd really give me something to worry about.'

'So, he threatened you?'

Sullivan bowed her head and nodded.

'Dear, dear,' said Munro. 'Why on earth did you not tell anyone?'

'I did.'

'The police?'

'No,' said Sullivan, 'that would've been suicide. I told Nick.'

Munro, buoyed by the fortuitous turn in the conversation, sat back and smiled graciously.

'That would be Mr Riley? The journalist?'

'It would. Now, how about that tea?'

'Aye, why not,' said Munro. 'Milk, three sugars.'

'We'll go outside, it's the only place that brings me peace.'

* * *

Standing on the patio with a tea in one hand and the other tucked behind his back, Munro – his spirits lifted by the abundance of pansies, violas, hydrangeas, and geraniums – gazed across the rambling garden and nodded approvingly at the weathered shiplap shed, its peeling, pale blue walls adorned with a collection of antique tools and an old advertising sign featuring two terriers extolling the virtues of Black & White whisky.

'Is this your work?' he said with an enthusiastic smile.

'Aye, it certainly is,' said Sullivan, 'and I've the scars to prove it.'

'You've a rare talent there, Miss Sullivan. A rare talent indeed. You're wasted behind a desk.'

'Tell me about it, but needs must, Mr Munro. When I went to art school my head was full of dreams. I was going to be the best illustrator this country had ever seen but life, as they say, doesn't always go according to plan.'

'More's the pity,' said Munro. 'Why did you not follow your dreams?'

'Things changed.'

'Changed?'

'Jessica,' said Sullivan. 'You can always count on kids to throw a spanner in the works. By the time she was five I was on my own, I had to take whatever job I could or starve.'

Inspired by Sullivan's effortless creativity compared to the unexciting layout of his own garden which, though home to a profuse amount of flowers and shrubs was best described as staid, Munro sipped his tea and pointed excitedly towards the shed.

'I'd never even thought of painting mine!' he said with an enthusiastic grin. 'Tell me, where on earth did you manage to get those things? I cannae see there being much demand for sickles and scythes these days.'

'Ebay,' said Sullivan, 'twenty quid the lot, and there's more in the shed.'

'Well it's a fine display, I'll give you that but, dinnae take this as a criticism, there's a wee gap on the end there. Could you not find something else to put up?'

'Oh, there's no gap,' said Sullivan. 'It's probably fallen off. There should be a rusty old billhook there. You can wander over and put it back if it's bothering you.'

'No, no. I'll not interfere with your handiwork. Tell me, Miss Sullivan, you and Mr Riley, I understand you shared a house together, is that right?'

'That's one way of putting it,' said Sullivan. 'We were engaged, Mr Munro. I couldn't have been happier, but then Jessica came along.'

'Jessica? Are you telling me that Mr Riley is Jessica's father?'

'He is indeed.'

'Then why is he not here now?'

'He didn't want kids. Too much responsibility he said. Not ready to settle down he said. Can't afford it he said.'

'The usual excuses.'

'Aye. Five years later I'd had enough. Jessica was old enough for nursery so I took myself off, found a wee job, and moved up here.'

'That was a brave move.'

'Brave or stupid,' said Sullivan. 'I'm still not sure which.'

'But in spite of Jessica, Mr Riley, he still has feelings for you?'

'Well if he has, he's not told me.'

'But you turned to him nonetheless when things became strained between yourself and Mr Ricci.'

'I did, aye,' said Sullivan. 'There was no-one else I could talk to.'

'And did he help?'

'Did he hell,' said Sullivan. 'I asked him, pleaded with him, for Jessica's sake, to have a word with Alex, give him a polite nudge, show him the door, but he refused.'

'Refused?'

'And that hurt more than anything else. You see, Jessica was the only reason we stayed in touch; he helped out, financially, I'll give him that. But it was like he wasn't bothered anymore, like he was trying to teach me a lesson, you know, you've made your bed, now lie in it.'

'That's very generous of the fellow.'

'Aye, isn't it just.'

'So, you were angry?'

'Angry's not the word,' said Sullivan. 'I was raging. All these years I'd been on my own, struggling to raise Jess, putting my own wants and needs on the back burner. I ask him for one lousy favour and he can't be arsed. I could've killed him.'

'So, you've not even had yourself a holiday?'

'You must be joking. I had a wee trip away after graduating and a week in Paris with Nick when we got engaged. The last twenty years I've been nowhere.'

'Dear, dear, I feel for you, Miss Sullivan, really I do, but tell me, do you not think the article Nick was writing was his way of helping? Of getting rid of Mr Ricci?'

'What article's that then?'

Munro glanced at Sullivan, finished his tea, and smiled.

'I'll get you a copy,' he said. 'You might see him in a different light once you've read it. I should be going.'

'Right you are,' said Sullivan. 'Thanks for dropping by. It's helped, you know, talking and stuff.'

'My pleasure,' said Munro. 'One thing, Miss Sullivan. When Mr Riley refused to help, what did you do?'

'What could I do? I prayed for karma, Mr Munro. And thank God someone was listening.'

Chapter 16

Pushing the boundaries of the video enhancement software to its very limits, Dougal – using all of his expertise to grab a half-decent image of Riley's attacker from the CCTV footage taken on Sandgate – beavered away in blissful silence while a sullen-faced West, looking as happy as a diabetic in a doughnut factory, sat with her feet on the desk staring glumly out of the window.

'I've seen happier folk at a requiem,' said Munro as he ambled through the door. 'What's the story?'

'The DNA on MacCall's flask,' said West. 'It's not Ricci.'

'Is that all?'

'Is that all!'

'There's more important things in life, Charlie.'

'I don't believe I'm hearing this.'

'Well if it's not Ricci,' said Munro, 'who is it?'

'God knows. Where have you been anyway?'

'Out. So, there's no match on the database?'

'To use a well-worn phrase, *it's unidentified.*'

'So, you're sitting around wasting precious time?'

'Actually no,' said West. 'We're waiting for a warrant to come through so we can go search Sullivan's gaff.'

'Is that so?'

'Yes it is. If we can't do him for topping MacCall, then we can do him for murdering Jessica Sullivan and assaulting Sophie Jackson. All we have to do is find the weapon he used to carve them up.'

'Good luck with that,' said Munro. 'Do you know what you're looking for?'

'If I told you,' said West, 'you'd only laugh.'

Spying two paper sacks and a clear, plastic bag lying on the desk, Munro, unable to resist, removed his jacket and eased himself into a chair.

'Who does this belong to?' he said, holding it aloft.

'Who do you think?' said West. 'The Italian Stallion.'

Curious, Munro prodded the bag with his forefinger as he analysed Ricci's possessions: a wallet, a set of house keys, a comb, a solid silver toothpick, a Rolex Oyster, a gold chain with a crucifix pendant, and a smartphone.

'Have you checked this?' he said.

'Aye, of course,' said Dougal. 'He's got MacCall's number on there but he's not been in touch since she left for Arran.'

Munro set the bag to one side and, peering into one of the paper sacks, ignored the screen-wipes, de-icer, sponge and squeegee which had obviously been retrieved from the boot of the Insignia, and turned his attention to the other.

Pulling on his spectacles and a pair of latex gloves, he tipped the contents to the desk and laid them in a straight line, inspecting each in turn like a thrifty collector at a bring-and-buy sale: one pair of sunglasses; two CDs, The Kaiser Chiefs and Andrea Bocelli; a make-up bag; a packet of travel tissues; and a hard-shell leather pouch.

'You're wasting your time,' said West. 'That's just a load of junk from the glove compartment. There's nothing there.'

'What's this?' said Munro as he unzipped the pouch.

'Oh, that's a suitably expensive manicure set, boss,' said Dougal. 'Giorgio Bagnara.'

'Is it indeed. In my experience, there's only one kind of a chap who uses a manicure set.'

'Who's that then?'

'One who doesnae want to get his hands dirty. Have these been dusted?'

'Aye, I think SOCOs took care of that.'

Munro removed the nail clippers and scrutinised the tips.

'We've not had a wee quiz for a while,' he said as he returned them to the pouch.

'Not now, Jimbo,' said West. 'I've got enough on my plate without you…'

'If I said *wood*, what would you say?'

Dougal, always game for a quiz, poked his head around the screen.

'Trees!' he yelped.

'Well done, laddie. And if I said *nose*?'

'Smell,' said West.

'Lose a point.'

'Under?' said Dougal.

Munro, apparently oblivious to Dougal's answer, toyed with an emery board then opened a pair of nail scissors and held them to the light.

'And if I said *none so blind*?'

'Those who cannot see!'

'We have a winner,' said Munro, placing the scissors atop the pouch. 'I've just come from seeing Helen Sullivan.'

'You what?' said West. 'What the hell were you doing there?'

Ignoring the question Munro continued as if talking to himself.

'Apparently Jessica Sullivan is Nick Riley's daughter…'

'What?'

'…and whoever attacked him didnae use a machete, not strictly speaking anyway. It was a billhook.'

West, completely shell-shocked, gawped at Dougal who, equally dumbstruck, sat with his chin on the floor.

'Okay,' she said, 'rewind a bit. Riley is Jessica's dad?'

'So Helen Sullivan claims.'

'Sorry, boss,' said Dougal, 'but how do you know it's a billhook?'

'I know because Helen Sullivan owns one.'

West stood up, ruffled her hair and groaned as she walked to the window.

'I'm going mad,' she said, raising her arms. 'Right, you two slow down a bit. First up, what the bleeding hell is a billhook?'

'It's like a machete,' said Dougal, 'but with a serrated edge. It's used for cutting back shrubbery, tall grass, that kind of thing.'

'Okay, second: what the heck has this got to do with Helen... oh wait a minute, are you trying to tell me that Helen Sullivan was the one who attacked Nick Riley?'

'That's exactly what I'm telling you,' said Munro. 'Do yourselves a favour and look at the film again. I think you'll find she's of a similar height and build to the assailant. And by the way, the billhook, it's an antique, so it'll not do much damage.'

West, beginning to believe that his recent erratic behaviour and absurd assumptions might be symptomatic of stage four dementia, glared at Munro and returned to her seat.

'Sorry, Jimbo,' she said. 'I just don't buy it.'

'Then you should ask her yourself, Charlie. She'll not hesitate in telling you, I'm sure.'

Munro heaved a sigh, hauled himself to his feet, and slung his coat over his shoulder.

'Have you heard of Yankee Doddle Dandy?' he said.

'Yeah, of course,' said West, 'he's the geezer who stuck a feather in his cap...'

'Well, there's one for yours,' said Munro, pointing at the desk. 'There's somewhere I have to be. If I'm not back, Charlie, I'll see you at yours.'

'Hold on, boss!' said Dougal as the door slammed shut. 'Oh, that's not fair. He's not told us the point of the quiz.'

West, rattled as to why someone like Munro who lived by the mantra *"a place for everything and everything in its place"* would leave the scissors on top of the pouch instead of replacing them, approached the desk and picked them up.

'Dougal,' she said, 'I need an FLS and a magnifier, now.'

* * *

Peering through a pair of orange goggles to filter out the blue channel from the spectrum, West directed the beam of the forensic light source over the splayed blades, turned to Dougal, and smiled.

'What is it?'

'Dead skin,' said West, 'and it looks like a spot of dried fluid too.'

'Jeez-oh!' said Dougal. 'That's a fast-track if ever I saw one.'

'You bag it up and I'll arrange a courier.'

'Courier? I'll not wait for them, miss. They'll be an age and the clock's ticking on Ricci as it is. No, no, I'll run it there myself.'

* * *

As Dougal thrashed his way along the A77 in a bid to reach Glasgow's Pacific Quay in less than forty-five minutes, West – her addled mind struggling to find a way of securing a conviction against Ricci not to mention her annoyance at Munro's eccentric if not blasé habit of unravelling a case like a ball of wool – dialled Mackenzie for an update on McIver's movements, only to be interrupted by the sound of boots thundering along the corridor.

'Miss!' yelled Duncan as he barged through the door. 'You're here! Good!'

'Where's the fire?' said West.

'Downstairs, and she's waiting for you.'

'Kirsty Young?'

'None other.'

'Okay, let me make this call first then we'll…'

'With all due respect miss,' said Duncan impatiently, 'we should go now. You'll not believe what she has to say.'

* * *

At five feet two inches tall, Kirsty Young – a gaunt nineteen year old, built like a string bean with straight brown hair, painted eyebrows, and cheeks as hollow as a politician's promise – could have saved herself a substantial fortune by shopping for her entire wardrobe in Mothercare or the children's section of any department store.

Swathed in an over-sized khaki puffa jacket with a voluminous hood, she sat with the look of a startled mouse, biting what was left of her fingernails as an ageing uniformed officer with a face like a bulldog watched her like a hawk.

Lifting a hand in a half-hearted wave, she mustered a tight-lipped smile and kept her eyes on Duncan as they filed through the door.

'Hello Kirsty,' said West as she sat behind the desk. 'How's it going?'

'Aye, okay.'

'Good. Has DC Reid offered you anything to drink?'

'He has.'

'Good. Now then, I gather there's something you've been wanting to tell us?'

'That's right.'

'So, what changed your mind? Let's face it, the last time we met you hardly said a word.'

'I heard what happened to Jessica Sullivan.'

West cocked her head and regarded her inquisitively.

'You knew Jessica Sullivan?'

'I did, aye. Not close, not like real pals, but we used to hang out at the same clubs.'

'So?'

'Folk are saying she was drugged.'

'I can't comment on that,' said West. 'I don't deal with gossip.'

'I know, but is that not what happened to Ella?'

West sat back, folded her arms, and raised her eyebrows.

'And how do you figure that?' she said. 'I don't recall anyone saying she'd been drugged.'

'No, I know,' said Kirsty, 'but something must have happened. I mean Ella's not the kind of girl to simply slip and hit her head, she's just too... careful. Sensible, you know?'

'Okay,' said West, 'let's pretend for a moment that she was. Drugged, I mean. How would that make a difference?'

'I'm not sure. I was just thinking that if she and Jessica, if they were attacked by the same person, then I'd not forgive myself if anything happened to someone else and I'd kept my mouth shut.'

'What about your pals?' said Duncan. 'Holly and Megan. Do they share your suspicions?'

'Probably, but they'll not speak up.'

'I can vouch for that. Why so? Why are they keeping quiet?'

'Too scared.'

'And do they know you're here?'

'No. And I don't want them to either.'

'Fair enough,' said West. 'So, you want to make a statement, is that it?'

'I just want to tell you what I know.'

West, more concerned with Dougal's progress than the testimony of a teenager who'd hitherto remained unaffected by her friend's premature death, cast a sideways glance at Duncan and stabbed the voice recorder.

'For the benefit of the tape,' she said, 'the time is 3:27 pm. I'm DI West, also present is DC Reid and Miss Kirsty Young. So, Kirsty, you want to talk to us about Ella MacCall, is that right?'

'It is, aye.'

'And is this concerning the events leading up to her death?'

'That's correct.'

'On you go,' said Duncan. 'There's nothing to worry about, hen, trust me.'

Kirsty paused and took a deep breath.

'I think I know who might be responsible.'

'Okay,' said Duncan, 'let me stop you there. Before you go on, do you realise how serious this is? I mean, you can't go making wild accusations based purely on a hunch, do you understand?'

Kirsty pursed her lips and nodded.

'Just to be clear then,' said West, searching for the missing part of the puzzle, 'did this person drive you and your friends from Kilmarnock to the Ormidale Hotel on Arran?'

'They did.'

'And was this someone involved in some sort of a relationship with Ella MacCall?'

'Most definitely, aye.'

Relieved to have finally found a witness who was willing to testify that their main suspect was indeed behind the wheel of the Vauxhall Insignia, West slumped in her seat back and smiled.

'Listen,' she said, 'just so you know, you're perfectly safe. Alessandro Ricci, *Alex*, is currently behind bars so there's absolutely no way he can get to you, okay?'

Kirsty, mystified by West's presumptuous yet mildly reassuring statement, frowned at Duncan before directing her gaze at West.

'Alex?' she said. 'No, no. See here, Inspector, you've got this all wrong. This has nothing to do with Alex.'

West, experiencing the kind of bowel movement normally associated with a plate of warm sashimi, sat bolt upright and glowered across the table.

'Well, if it's not Ricci,' she said, 'then who the hell is it?'

'Isla,' said Kirsty. 'Isla Thomson.'

Stupefied by the allegation, West, maintaining her composure, slowly stood, slipped her hands into her pockets and leaned against the wall.

'Isla Thomson?' she said cynically. 'And is this the same Isla Thomson who teaches PE on Arran?'

'Aye, that's right.'

'The same Isla Thomson who's a volunteer with mountain rescue?'

'Aye,' said Kirsty, 'and it's the same Isla Thomson who coaches hockey, and it's the same Isla Thomson who's been dating Ella for over a year.'

'Hold on,' said Duncan, 'are you saying Ella and Isla were…'

'Oh come on, we're not in the dark ages.'

'No, no, I didn't mean it like that. I just didn't see that coming, that's all. So, what happened?'

'Usual story,' said Kirsty. 'A bust-up. Ella finished with her. Well, she tried to anyway.'

'When?'

'Can't say for sure. A few weeks, maybe.'

'And do you know why?'

'Ella said Thomson was a control freak with a temper and a half. She let it go at first seeing as how Isla was that much older than her but then she got scared, and rightly so. I mean, you've seen her, she's strong. I know a few fellas she could fell with a single punch.'

'Did she have a history of violence against Ella?' said West. 'Did she ever hit her?'

'No, not that I know of. But she was that fed up, she was bordering on depression.'

'How bad?'

'Bad enough.'

'Was she suicidal?'

'Not far off it,' said Kirsty, 'but Isla told her she was projecting, blaming their relationship for other stuff that was wrong with her life. She even gave her some pills, you know, anti-depressants. She said they'd help her sleep better.'

'When did you find out she was taking pills?'

'The first I heard was when she called me from the hospital, she'd taken a tumble and fallen in the harbour.'

'In Troon?'

'Aye, that's right. She said she thought she was losing her marbles because she couldn't even remember going there.'

'Listen, hen,' said Dougal, 'you're into social media, right? Did you know Ella had a Facebook page?'

'I did, but it's not hers, not really.'

'How do you mean?'

'Ella was never into stuff like that,' said Kirsty. 'Isla set it up for her.'

'But you've seen the wee videos on there?'

'I have.'

'And do you know who filmed them?'

'I'm guessing Thomson.'

'Not your pal Alex?'

'No, you'd never get the three of them together.'

'The thing is,' said West, 'why would Ella post a film of her falling in the drink for all the world to gloat at?'

'Like I said, she didn't. Truth is, Inspector, I doubt Ella even knew they were there.'

Having experienced first-hand the psychological trauma of a coercive relationship, West – though touched by empathy for Ella MacCall – could not justify jealousy as a reasonable excuse for Thomson's behaviour and remained doubtful of her culpability.

'Okay,' she said, becoming bored by what was beginning to sound like an extract from an agony aunt column, 'so Isla Thomson wasn't happy about being given the heave-ho. Frankly, I don't see why it's such a big deal.'

'Oh, you're not listening, are you?' said Kirsty. 'She wasn't unhappy, she was raging! She was that possessive, she just couldn't handle not being in control.'

'Possessive?' said Duncan. 'How so?'

'She'd not let Ella out of her sight if she could help it. They had to talk on the phone every evening if they weren't together and she even did her best to keep us apart. She told her that if she ever left, if she ever found someone else, then she'd be sorry.'

'Well why did Ella not get some help? Some counselling maybe?'

'She did,' said Kirsty. 'She talked to Alex. He was a *grown-up*, she said. She figured he'd protect her and get Thomson off her back.'

'But it didn't work out that way, did it?' said West.

'No, it did not,' said Kirsty. 'Thomson's not a dafty, Inspector. She knew full-well what Ella was up to, so she got pally with Alex; she was trying to drive a wedge between them, make her jealous so she'd come back.'

'So, you're convinced Thomson was responsible for Ella's death?'

'Aye, I'm certain of it.'

'Okay. And how do you think she did it?'

Kirsty held West's gaze for just a second, then lowered her head.

'I'm not sure,' she said sheepishly. 'All I know is, Ella may have been fed up but she'd not kill herself.'

'Well, I'm sorry,' said West, 'but don't you think it's a bit extreme? The old "if I can't have you, nobody will"?'

'Not with Thomson, no. She's a psycho. See here, Inspector, even on the journey over she and Ella never said a single word to each other. Not a word. Until Ella said we were thinking about taking a walk up Goat Fell.'

'Hang on,' said West perking up. 'You mean she didn't try to stop you?'

'Did she hell,' said Kirsty. 'When Megan and I said we were having second thoughts because it looked like snow was on the way, Thomson said we were acting like a couple of lightweights. She said she knew the mountain like the back of her hand. She said she knew how the weather would turn. She said by the time we got a mile or two up the path, the cloud would lift and we'd be on our way.'

'But she didn't go with you?'

'Oh no,' said Kirsty, 'but get this. That afternoon she shows up and she's all sweetness and light, smiling and chatting to Ella like nothing was wrong. She even brought us a map with the path highlighted in marker pen, then stood there sharing a flask of soup before giving it to Ella and sending us on our way.'

West, postulating that the mention of the flask might lend some credence to her story, pushed herself off the wall and, deep in thought, walked heel to toe around the room.

'What was your relationship with Isla Thomson, Kirsty?' she said.

'Are you joking me? I'm not that way inclined. And even if I was, she's not my type.'

'No. I mean in general. How did you two get on?'

'We didn't. We exchanged pleasantries, that was it.'

'So, you've no reason to feel vindictive towards her?'

'I have not.'

'She's never crossed you? Upset you? Threatened you?'

'No, never. Why?'

'Because,' said West, 'there's one thing I can't fathom out. One thing that doesn't quite add up.'

'What's that then?'

'You say Isla Thomson drove you, Ella and your friends from Ardrossan and dropped you all at the Ormidale Hotel.'

'That's right, aye.'

'In a silver Vauxhall?'

'Correct.'

'That car belongs to Alessandro Ricci's partner, Helen Sullivan.'

'I wouldn't know about that,' said Kirsty, 'all I know is, I've seen Alex driving it about the place.'

'So how did Thomson get her hands on it?'

'She borrowed it off Alex.'

'Where was her car?'

'At home,' said Kirsty. 'It's too small for all of us to fit in so she got a lift to hockey with a pal of hers from some garage on Arran, then drove us back in the Vauxhall after practice.'

'I need to be crystal clear about this, Kirsty,' said West. 'You're absolutely sure it was Isla Thomson who drove you off the ferry and dropped you at the hotel?'

'Aye, of course, that's what I've been saying all along.'

'Well, here's the thing, sweetheart,' said Duncan. 'Isla didn't go back to Ardrossan that night. She stayed on Arran. So how do you think that car got all the way back to the mainland?'

'Is that all that's bothering you?'

'It's a big *all*,' said West.

'Thomson drove it back onto the ferry then hopped off,' said Kirsty. 'Alex picked it up when it docked in Ardrossan.'

Conscious of the fact that her impetuous behaviour was behind a raft of snap decisions and rash judgements which had hitherto blighted her career, West – gambling on upping her success rate – walked briskly back to the desk.

'I've got a call to make,' she said, her finger hovering above the stop button. 'Interview terminated. The time is 3:55 pm.'

'Terminated? But what about me?' said Kirsty as West disappeared through the door. 'I'll not go home. What if Isla...'

'Don't you worry, hen,' said Duncan. 'We'll sort you out.'

* * *

Pausing on the landing of the concrete stairwell, West pulled her phone from the holster and hit redial.

'Hello, Inspector,' said Mackenzie. 'And how are you?'

'No time for that,' said West, her voice bouncing off the walls. 'There's something I need you to do.'

'Is this about the email?'

'What email?'

'The one I sent this afternoon,' said Mackenzie. 'John McIver. He was booked on the 11:05 this morning. Arrived Ardrossan midday.'

'So, where the hell has he gone?'

'I've really no idea.'

'Has he got family or friends on the mainland?'

'Not unless you count the fellas at the motor spares depot.'

'Well, he must know someone,' said West. 'Ask around, I don't give a monkey's if everyone's sick to death of talking to you, I need to know where he's gone.'

'I'll do my best. Is that it?'

'Not by a long chalk. Isla Thomson.'

'Oh aye. Are you still chasing her?'

'Not any more,' said West. 'You are.'

'I'm not with you.'

'I want you to arrest her on suspicion of the murder of Miss Ella MacCall.'

'Are you serious?'

'Deadly. I need her dabs uploaded and a DNA swab as soon as you've nicked her. And don't forget to bring it with you.'

'No disrespect,' said Mackenzie, 'but are you sure about this? I mean, this is Isla Thomson we're talking about here.'

'Just do as you're bloody well told,' said West. 'There's a ferry at 4:40, make sure you're on it.'

Waiting until she'd finished her conversation, Duncan – hovering a few steps down – glanced up at her and frowned.

'Miss?'

'Thomson should be on the next ferry over.'

'So, we're going with it?'

'We have to,' said West, a distant look of bewilderment in her eyes.

'But?'

'But if Thomson did spike MacCall's flask, where the hell did she lay her hands on the drug?'

'Oh, I'm sure if the scallies on the streets can get hold of it, miss, then she probably can.'

'Yeah, maybe,' said West. 'Maybe.'

'What will we do with Kirsty?'

'You sort it. I'll be upstairs.'

Chapter 17

Unaccustomed to the formalities of meetings or interviews with anyone but the bank manager, John McIver – a self-taught, self-employed, and self-assured singleton with an undeniable talent for mending and maintaining anything of a mechanical nature – felt as nervous as a canary in a coal mine as he wandered around the empty office waiting for someone to arrive.

Unsure whether to stand or sit, he flinched, ducking instinctively as West, puffing from a sprint up the stairs, burst through the door.

'Well, well, well,' she said, catching her breath, 'if it isn't the elusive Mr McIver.'

'He said it was okay to come up.'

'Who did?'

'The fella downstairs,' said McIver, removing his cap. 'I told him you were expecting me, I hope that's okay.'

'He's a got a cheek,' said West. 'Security's bad enough as it is without some halfwit allowing a suspected murderer to wander about the place.'

'Sorry?'

West regarded McIver as if she'd just been roused from the midst of a particularly unpleasant dream.

'Ignore me,' she said, shaking her head. 'How can I help?'

'I've no idea,' said McIver. 'Bobby, that is, PC Mackenzie, he left me a message. He said you were wanting a word with me.'

'Oh yeah,' said West, 'so I was. It doesn't matter now, you're off the hook.'

'What hook?'

'Forget it,' said West as she checked her watch. 'You can go. Sorry you've had a wasted journey.'

'Oh, it's not wasted,' said McIver, 'I'm here to collect some stock and I'm stopping over too. I thought I'd have myself a few bevvies and a bite to eat.'

'Good for you.'

McIver, hovering as if hankering after an invitation to stay, finally turned for the door.

'Okay,' he said, 'that's me away then. Cheery-bye, Inspector.'

'Yeah, bye-bye,' said West flippantly when, in a rare moment of lucidity, she remembered his prescription. 'John! John, come back!'

McIver poked his head round the door and smiled.

'There is something after all,' said West, 'come in and take a pew.'

'Okey-dokey,' said McIver, ogling her tight T-shirt and figure-hugging jeans. 'Is this about tonight? Because if it's company you're after I've no plans. Not really.'

'Oh please,' said West as Duncan returned. 'Thanks but I'm working late. Fancy a cuppa?'

'Aye, go on then.'

'Duncan, stick the kettle on, would you?'

'No bother. Mr McIver, how's yourself?'

'Not bad, Constable. You?'

'Aye, all good. Milk and sugar?'

McIver nodded as West perched herself on the desk opposite.

'You take stuff to help you sleep, don't you, Mr McIver?' she said.

'I do,' said McIver. 'It's not a regular thing. I only take it if I have to. Mostly after a call-out or like tonight, here in town. I can't take the noise.'

'Yeah, yeah, I'm not bothered about that,' said West waving her arm. 'Remind me again, what is it you're on?'

'Flunitrazepam.'

'Rohypnol, Miss,' said Duncan. 'That's the same stuff...'

'That's enough,' said West. 'Mr McIver, if I remember correctly, when we met you said you'd just collected a new batch from your GP. Is that right?'

'Aye, absolutely. I was in a rush, mind, to make the surgery before it closed. That was some dash off the ferry, I can tell you.'

'And then you went home?'

'No, no. I headed back to the garage to lock up.'

'Was anyone there?'

'Only Isla. She was tanking up a customer for me.'

'And were you there long?'

'Oh, about a quarter of an hour,' said McIver. 'Twenty minutes tops.'

'And where did you leave your pills?'

'In my coat.'

'And your coat was where?'

'Oh, now you're asking. On the bench maybe. Or in the office. That's where I keep the cash when I lock up.'

'And did Isla wait for you?' said West. 'I mean, did you leave together?'

'Let me think. No, as I recall I was bolting the doors at the back of the workshop when she shouted to say she was off.'

West paused for a moment, sipped her tea, and stared at McIver.

'This new pack of tabs,' she said. 'Have you taken any yet?'

'No, no. But I'll be needing one tonight, that's for sure.'

'So you've got them with you?'

'Oh aye,' said McIver as he reached into his pocket. 'Would you like a wee look?'

McIver sat back and laughed as West, much to his amusement, pulled on a pair of gloves.

'I've not got anything contagious,' he said. 'You'll not catch anything off there.'

West glanced up and smiled politely.

'Thirty tablets,' she said as she opened the carton. 'Three strips of ten, right?'

'Aye, that's right.'

'And you've not taken any?'

'If I had, my head would be on the desk.'

'Then why,' said West holding up a strip,' are there three missing?'

'Dear, dear,' said McIver, unfazed by her discovery. 'Not again.'

'Again? You mean this has happened before?'

'A few times, aye. It's not right. I told my GP but she said it's likely to be a glitch at the factory.'

'Hell of a glitch,' said West. 'Listen, what time do you go to bed?'

McIver's mischievous smile dissipated as he locked eyes with West.

'Ten,' he said, clearing his throat. 'I shall be in my pit by ten.'

'Good. I need to hang on to these. I'll get them back to you in a couple of hours. Where are you staying?'

'The Beechwood on Prestwick Road.'

'Thanks. Now drink up. I've got work to do.'

West handed Duncan the carton as McIver, feeling as confused as a chameleon in a kaleidoscope, shuffled from the room.

'Get this dusted,' she said, 'if there's anything there, it'll be on that strip and with any luck it'll belong to you know who.'

'Roger that, miss.'

'By the way, what have you done with Kirsty?'

'Holiday Inn and twenty quid to fetch herself some dinner.'

'That's generous of you.'

'Not really,' said Duncan. 'It's all going on expenses.'

* * *

Jaundiced by the dim glow of the harbour lights, West – leaning on the bonnet of the Defender – nodded as Mackenzie strolled towards them like an agent arriving at Checkpoint Charlie ready to exchange a couple of spooks.

Ignoring the inquisitive glances of the other passengers, she watched as he placed his hand on Thomson's head and eased her into the rear of one of two patrol cars parked alongside.

'You okay?' said Duncan. 'You look frazzled.'

'It's not easy,' said Mackenzie. 'Arresting a friend, it just doesn't feel right.'

'Get over it pal. If she's not guilty, she'll be back tomorrow.'

'Ignore him,' said West, stifling a smile. 'He's just hacked off because we've not had lunch. Prints?'

'Aye, all done,' said Mackenzie as he pulled a small jiffy bag from his tunic pocket. 'And this is the swab.'

'Nice one, Constable. So, what does the night hold in store for you?'

'Not much. I'm back on board that thing. She'll sail in twenty minutes and if I'm not on it, that's me humped. There'll not be another until the morning.'

Leaving the driver of the second patrol car with the DNA sample and strict instructions to ask for DS Dougal McCrae when he got to Pacific Quay, Duncan – dreading the ride back in the dilapidated Defender – buttoned his coat against the impending chill.

'How long's that going to take?' said West as the blue lights faded into the distance.

'Well, if he gives it some wellie, miss, I'd say he could do it in half an hour. Maybe less.'

'Good. So, if we're lucky, by the time we've given Thomson a good grilling, we could have a result.'

'Aye, maybe,' said Duncan as he fastened his safety belt. 'Talking of grilling, miss, are you thinking what I'm thinking?'

'Large kebab, onions, chilli sauce?'

'Oh, you're on the money there. I think I could probably go a wee shish too.'

'Sorry, big boy, but you're going to have to wait. Let's get Thomson sorted first, then remind me to ring Jimbo. He's acting odd and I'm not sure I like it.'

Chapter 18

Isla Thomson, an irascible individualist whose adherence to rules and regulations, implied or otherwise, was strictly limited to the highway code, ignored the vacant chair and, perspiring gently as the deafening silence and interminable wait fuelled her anxiety, paced the perimeter of the interview room like a rat trapped in cage.

'Thanks for dropping by,' said West as she breezed through the door.

'It's not as if I had a say in the matter, is it?'

'No. I suppose not. Have a seat.'

'I'd rather not,' said Thomson, glowering across the room. 'I'm not stopping. Not only have I been dragged here against my will, I've been arrested for a murder I know nothing about.'

'You've been arrested on *suspicion* of murder,' said West. 'They're two different things. Now sit down.'

'I'm quite happy where I am.'

'I said sit. Now, before we have a little chat, have you called your solicitor?'

'If it's just a wee chat you're after,' said Thomson sarcastically, 'I'll not be needing one.'

'I'd think twice about that if I were you,' said West. 'I can send for the duty solicitor if you'd like.'

'The innocent don't need defending.'

'You're so right,' said West. 'And are you?'

'Am I what?'

'Innocent.'

'As the day is long.'

'Good,' said West. 'I'm glad to hear it, because if that's the case you'll be out of here in a flash. If you're lucky, you might even get a lift home with your mate McIver.'

Thomson, driving her hands into the pockets of her fleece, stepped forward and sat down.

'John?' she said. 'Is he here?'

'Oh yeah. In fact, we've just had a lovely little natter about stuff.'

'What stuff?'

'Oh, you know: work, dinner, death, insomnia.'

'I'm not with you.'

'You soon will be,' said West as she started the voice recorder. 'For the benefit of the tape, the time is 6:29 pm. I am Detective Inspector West. Would you please state your name?'

'Thomson. Isla Thomson.'

'And do you understand why you're here, Miss Thomson?'

'Aye. Because whoever's in charge of this case has made a monumental cock-up.'

'Good. Let's start with Alessandro Ricci, shall we? Also known as Alex Ricci. When did you two first meet?'

'I don't remember.'

'Was it when he arrived at the community sports centre to discuss a sponsorship deal with your hockey team?'

'Maybe.'

'Well, you obviously hit it off,' said West. 'Why was that? Did you fancy him?'

'Are you joking me?' said Thomson. 'No. I did not.'

'Then why did you go out of your way to strike up a friendship? If it wasn't a mutual attraction…'

'No comment.'

'…then perhaps it was because you were jealous. Jealous that your mate Ella MacCall had taken a shine to him.'

'She did not.'

'Really?' said West. 'That's not what I've heard. I've been told they got quite… what's the word? *Close*. But let's not dwell on that now, it's obviously upsetting you, thinking about your partner getting flirty with somebody else. Let's move on. Let's talk about Ella instead. How long have you two been seeing each other?'

Thomson, her face as frozen as a Hollywood has-been with a faceful of Botox, gazed unflinchingly at West.

'No comment,' she said.

Surprised that somebody like Thomson whose entire career was built around socially interactive pursuits had yet to master the art of conversation, West – mildly irritated at her reluctance to answer any questions in words of more than two syllables – left her seat and ambled slowly back and forth behind the desk.

'I was in a relationship with this bloke once,' she said as if musing on her past. 'Everything was great to start with but when the sparks stopped flying, he couldn't wait to get out. Is that what happened with you and Ella? Did the fire go out?'

'No comment.'

'The thing is, you still fancied the pants off her, didn't you? Loved her even. But she didn't feel the same, did she?'

Thomson rolled her eyes and sighed.

'So you hounded her. Threatened her. Tormented her. Made her life a living hell.'

'I did not!' said Thomson as her blood began to boil. 'She was confused! She had baggage. Emotional baggage. It was clouding her judgement.'

'Bet those clouds weren't as bad as the ones up the top of Goat Fell though, were they?' said West. 'Still, you must have found some compassion for her somewhere, after all, you drove her and her mates all the way from Kilmarnock to Arran for their holiday. And not only that, you even made her a lovely flask of soup for her trek up the mountain, didn't you?'

'Are we done here?' said Thomson as her temper frayed, 'because so far you've not said anything that...'

Thomson's words tailed off as West, interrupted by the ping of her phone, raised a hand, read a brief text from Duncan, and smiled at the inclusion of a laughing emoji.

'Sorry about that,' she said. 'It's just work. Now, where were we? Oh yeah. Facebook. Let's talk about Facebook. I've got zero interest in it myself. Ella strikes me as the kind of girl who wouldn't be interested in it either. What do you think?'

'She wasn't,' said Thomson with a huff. 'She was like me. She had no time for all that internet stuff. She loved her sports and the outdoors.'

'Then why did she have a Facebook page? I can only imagine somebody did it for her.'

Thomson, twitching in her seat as the walls closed in, glanced furtively around the room.

'Yes. That'll be it,' West said. 'Someone must've done it for her.'

She returned to her seat, leaned across the table, and clasped her hands beneath her chin.

'We've got a bloke upstairs,' she said, smiling softly, 'he's a right whizz on computers, he is. Blinding, in fact. He knows all about IP addresses and protocols, in fact, if somebody sends us an anonymous email, he can tell us where it came from, just like that.'

Thomson's shoulders sagged as she nervously scratched the back of her head.

'We did it,' she said. 'I did it.'

'Well, well. An admission. So why did you put her on Facebook?'

'Alex suggested it. He said we should raise her profile, get her noticed. Maybe see if she didn't get snapped up by one of the better teams.'

'Really?' said West. 'Well, if you don't mind me saying so, I think you've missed a trick there. You've gone about it all the wrong way, I mean, there's absolutely nothing on there about her. No biography, nothing about her playing skills, there's not even a film of her in action. Just a few weird films of her stepping out in front of a car and falling into a harbour, stuff like that. All a bit bizarre, really.'

'I wouldn't know about that,' said Thomson. 'Maybe she posted them herself.'

'Nah, I mean, how would that work?' said West. 'How could she possibly film herself while she was carrying out those silly stunts? It's impossible. Besides, I just don't think it's the kind of thing a sensible girl like Ella would do. Not unless she'd been drugged.'

Thomson unzipped her fleece and coughed politely into her hand.

'Drugged?' she said. 'That's ridiculous.'

'Is it? Sorry, I'm not playing fair, am I? I think I should tell you that we know it was you who uploaded those films...'

'Rubbish!'

'...in fact,' said West as she produced Thomson's mobile phone, 'we know it was you who filmed her, because they're on here.'

'Hey you!' said Thomson. 'Just you hold on a minute! I know my rights, you need my permission to look at that!'

'I know. I forgot. Still, you don't mind, do you? Nah, didn't think you did.'

Thomson reared up in her seat and jabbed a finger at West.

'You think you're clever, don't you?' she said, raising her voice. 'Well, you're not that smart! Just where do you think I'd get my hands on some drugs, least of all roofies! It's a prescription drug! I couldn't get it without a prescription!'

West leaned back, folded her arms and, savouring the moment, smiled contentedly.

'Thanks for that,' she said. 'You've just saved me a whole lot of trouble.'

'Oh aye?' said Thomson. 'How so?'

'By incriminating yourself, of course. I didn't say she was drugged with Rohypnol, did I? Or Flunitrazepam. In fact, I haven't even mentioned Benzos at all.'

'Lucky guess,' said Thomson. 'That's what they use to spike drinks, isn't it?'

'Who said her drink was spiked?'

'I don't know where you're going with this,' said Thomson, 'but you can't prove a damned thing! I don't care what you think, or what you say, there's no way I could've got hold of that stuff.'

'John McIver knows where you got hold of it.'

Thomson, frowning as the conversation took a turn for the worse, glared at West.

'John?'

'Yup. He's had his tabs go missing for a while now.'

'Well that's nothing to do with me.'

'No? Then how come your fingerprints were on the packet of pills he got from his GP?'

'Don't be daft.'

'That message I just got,' said West. 'That was to confirm your dabs were found on a box of Rohypnol that John McIver had yet to open.'

'Circumstantial,' said Thomson. 'I must've picked them up and moved them.'

'Of course you did. And no doubt you accidentally opened the pack and a handful of pills just happened to fall out.'

'So, what now? Are you charging me with something?'

'No, not yet,' said West. 'I'm still waiting for the icing to arrive. For your cake, that is. In the meantime, I'm going to hold you just a little bit longer.'

'You can't do that!' said Thomson. 'I've already been here for…'

'Oh but I can,' said West. 'So, you go have a lie-down and I'll be back in a bit.'

* * *

Attributing her acerbic if not bullish behaviour in the interview room to a temporary hormonal imbalance or the imminent arrival of a full moon rather than a surge of confidence precipitated by Thomson's floundering defence, West – concerned that her fingerprints alone may not be enough to secure a conviction – scraped her hair back, pinned it atop her head, and sighed as she rifled through the cupboards for something to eat.

'Are you okay?' said Duncan.

'Not really,' said West as she eyed a stale ginger nut. 'My head's spinning.'

'Aye, I get what you mean. First we've nothing, then boom! It all comes together! It's all a bit much to take in.'

'What the hell are you jabbering on about?'

'Isla Thomson of course!'

'It's nothing to do with Isla Thomson,' said West, 'I'm talking blood sugar. I'm flipping starving.'

'Will I fetch us those kebabs?'

'No, ta. You go ahead if you like. To be honest, I've got to the stage where a large Balvenie seems more important.'

'Okay, if you're sure.'

'I am,' said West as she answered the phone. 'Dougal! What's up?'

'I've been trying to reach you for ages, miss!'

'Sorry, mate, I've been tied up with that mountain-climbing PE teacher.'

'It's her I need to talk to you about, you'd best get the champagne on ice!'

'Champagne?'

'Aye, but not for me, I'll take a grape juice if we've any in the fridge.'

'Does this mean you've got good news?'

'Better than good,' said Dougal. 'We ran Thomson's DNA through the database, it's a match positive for the unidentified DNA on MacCall's flask.'

West, her ears ringing with the sound of a nail being hammered into a coffin, turned to Duncan and smiled.

'Did you hear that?' she said. 'It's Thomson's DNA on the flask.'

'Result, miss!' said Duncan. 'That's her away then, you must be well chuffed.'

'I'm so happy I could crush you with a bear hug.'

'Not necessary, miss. Really. Not necessary.'

'Well?' said West, 'What are you waiting for?'

'Sorry?'

'Are you going to do the honours or what?'

'You mean charge her?'

'Well, I can't, I'm on the phone.'

'Roger that, miss, it'll be a pleasure.'

'Dougal, are you miles away or should we hang on?'

'No, no, miss! You hang on! I've another surprise for you.'

'I hope it's nothing fancy,' said West. 'I need to get going soon and besides, I'm not one for surprises. I've had far too many of those recently.'

'Oh, you'll like this one,' said Dougal. 'In fact, is the boss there? He'll like this too.'

'Jimbo? Christ, no! And I'm meant to call him. Put your foot down Dougal, quick as you can.'

* * *

As a reclusive maverick who'd spent his entire career shunning publicity – even declining a commendation for fear of having his face plastered all over the local press – Munro, embarrassed by the shrill shriek of his phone and the disparaging glances of those nearby, slinked from view and, after a cursory glance over his shoulder, reluctantly took the call.

'Charlie!' he said gruffly. 'It's not a good time.'

'Why? Are you driving?'

'No, I'm walking down the aisle.'

'Ding-dong! You're not talking wedding bells, are you?'

'Indeed I am not! I'm talking beers, wines, and spirits.'

'That's my boy! Hang on, surely you're not back in Carsethorn already?'

'No,' said Munro. 'I had an appointment to keep and I am currently shopping for groceries. I'll see you at yours.'

'Does this mean you're cooking?'

'I certainly am, so dinnae drag your heels. A veritable feast awaits.'

'Good,' said West, 'because not only am I starving, we've got cause to celebrate too.'

'How so?'

'Isla Thomson. She's going down for the murder of Ella MacCall.'

'Well done, Charlie! That is good news. Assuming she's guilty, of course.'

* * *

With details of MacCall's death already before the Fiscal and Thomson destined for a day in court, Duncan – an advocate of the Biblical saying that 'man shall not live by bread alone' – groaned as any thoughts he'd had of a spicy shish vanished into thin air whilst an excitable Dougal, prancing about like a dancer auditioning for the lead in *Billy Elliot*, struggled to contain himself.

'For God's sake!' said West. 'Calm down and take your flipping coat off!'

'We haven't time, miss!' said Dougal. 'I've got back-up waiting downstairs!'

'Duncan, give the man a paper bag, I think he's hyper-ventilating. What took you so long? Where have you been?'

'I stopped off at Helen Sullivan's, I'll explain on the way.'

'Just you hold your horses,' said West. 'Now, one step at a time, what are you so excited about?'

'Okay,' said Dougal taking a long, deep breath. 'Here's the thing. The manicure set. The nail scissors in the manicure set. There were samples of skin tissue and plasma on the blades.'

'Yeah, yeah, we figured that!' said West. 'Get on with it!'

'It belongs to Jessica Sullivan...'

'Well, we assumed that anyway! Blimey, I thought you were going to tell us something we didn't know!'

'I am! There were also fingerprints on the nail clippers, and the tweezers, and the case.'

'Woo-hoo!' said West, punching the air. 'That's Ricci banged to rights, then! Get in there! Double-top!'

'No, no,' said Dougal. 'You're wide of the mark there, miss. The fingerprints, they're not Ricci's. They belong to Nick Riley.'

West, looking as though she'd taken a body blow to the breadbasket, gawped at Dougal with a look of utter disbelief.

'You know how to take the wind out of a girl's sails, don't you?'

'That's not all,' said Dougal as he zipped his jacket. 'Have you got any aspirin with you?'

'No, why? Have you got a headache?'

'No. But you will have. Any second now. When they ran Sullivan's DNA through the DB it kicked up two matches.'

'Two?' said West, 'but that's... oh, hold on, you had me worried there for a moment. Nick Riley, right? I mean, he's her old man.'

189

'Not according to the DNA, he's not. Alessandro Ricci is.'

Chapter 19

As a tomboy growing up in the backwoods of Berkshire, West – who could scale a tree with the agility of an ape and fail an exam without putting pen to paper – had always considered the countryside of the home counties to be nothing less than idyllic until, staring down Bath Place through the windscreen of the Defender with nothing ahead but the open sea rippling beneath a vast night sky, she realised just how riddled with light pollution the south really was.

'Do you know something?' she said. 'The last time I saw a sky as black as that was during a power-cut.'

'Oh, it's even better when it's blowing a hoolie, miss. Then you've got the waves crashing onto the beach as well. It's quite a sight.'

'I've never seen so many stars. Ever.'

'Aye well,' said Dougal. 'The streets of London may be paved with gold, but we've got the diamonds, that's for sure.'

West heaved a contented sigh and glanced across at the house.

'Right,' she said, 'let's not waste any more time, my dinner's going cold. You've been dealing with this Riley geezer, Dougal, it's your call, just fill me in.'

'Okay,' said Dougal, 'so as I said, I called in on Sullivan on the way back. Now if you remember she'd told the boss…'

'Jimbo?'

'Aye. She'd said that Nick Riley was Jessica's father and that he'd walked out not long after she was born because he didn't want to have kids. Not so. You see, Helen Sullivan first met Alessandro Ricci nearly twenty years ago…'

'I can see where this is going.'

'…when she spent an entire summer at the Siena Art Institute. She came back here and hey presto, nine months later…'

'But Riley was having none of it,' said West. 'He knew Jessica wasn't his and that's why he left.'

'Exactly, miss. Then after all the hoo-ha he went through at home, Ricci pitches up out of the blue…'

'And Riley sees red.'

'…which explains why he and Sullivan shacked up together so soon after getting re-acquainted.'

'So Riley gets wind of this and decides to nail him once and for all. Set him up. Frame him.'

'That's how it looks.'

Leaning on the steering wheel with her chin on her hands, West – mesmerised by the distant lights of a trawler bobbing across the Firth – remained anxious, despite the evidence, about arresting Riley unless the case against him was absolutely watertight.

'I've got every faith in you Dougal,' she said, 'but we have to watch we don't trip ourselves up.'

'How so?'

'One tiny thing. The manicure set. How did it end up in Sullivan's motor?'

'I think I've got that covered,' said Dougal. 'Will we go?'

* * *

Accustomed to spending his evenings alone with a six pack of Stella and a curry flavour Pot Noodle, Riley, clutching a can of lager, padded down the hall in his stockinged feet and peered cautiously through the glass before opening the door.

'Mr Riley,' said Dougal. 'I see you've lost the sling.'

'It's not worth the trouble, Sergeant. Oh, Inspector, I see you're here too. To what do I owe the pleasure?'

'We need a word,' said West. 'Mind if we come in?'

'If you must.'

Riley took a swig of beer, wiped his mouth with the back of his hand, and led them to the lounge.

'I'd offer you a tea or a coffee,' he said as he slumped on the sofa, 'but frankly I can't be bothered.'

'No worries,' said West. 'This won't take long. It's about your ex, Helen Sullivan.'

'Oh aye? What about her?'

'We thought you'd like to know that we won't be doing her for possession of an offensive weapon....'

'I'm not sure I follow.'

'...but she'd like to know if you're going to press charges.'

'Charges? What are you havering about? What charges?'

'Well the most obvious one would be assault,' said West. 'Or to be more precise, GBH with intent.'

'I see,' said Riley. 'So, you know it was her?'

'What do you think?'

'The woman's demented. A bampot. She needs locking up.'

'Why the charade?' said Dougal. 'If you knew it was Helen who'd assaulted you, then why were you so keen for us to believe it was Alessandro Ricci?'

'He needed to be taught a lesson.'

'How so?'

'For taking advantage.'

'Of who?'

'Those girls in Italy.'

'Those girls?' said Dougal. 'Or one girl in particular?'

Riley, undaunted by the question, calmly crossed his legs, swilled the beer round the can, and took a large gulp.

'So,' said West. 'Are you going to press charges?'

'No.'

'Well, we've got a few we're going to throw at you.'

'Me?'

'Yup. We'll start with perverting the course of justice,' said West, 'then there's that old favourite, wasting police time and, oh, before I forget, you might like to know that Alessandro Ricci is considering suing you for defamation.'

Riley finished his beer, crushed the can, and laughed.

'He's going to do that from his cell, is he? Very good, Inspector. Very good indeed.'

'He'll not be in a cell,' said Dougal.

'What do you mean?'

'We can't put him in a cell if he's done nothing wrong.'

'Have you lost your mind?' said Riley. 'Nothing wrong? The man's guilty of murder!'

'Is he?'

'Aye! Jessica! And he attacked her pal too!'

'What makes you say that?' said West. 'I mean, what makes you think Alessandro Ricci had anything to do with the assault on those girls?'

'The inspector's right,' said Dougal. 'Your imagination's running away with you, Mr Riley. Best take it easy on the ale, eh?'

'Don't patronise me!' said Riley. 'Good God! Are you that stupid? Of course it was him! Have you forgotten about the tattoos!'

'Oh aye, of course. The tattoos.'

'*Vixi*,' said Riley. 'It's the same phrase he inscribed on his victims in Italy! Now you tell me, who else could have done that?'

'Who indeed?' said Dougal, frowning as he scratched the back of his neck. 'It's a question I asked myself many times over until we discovered what the perpetrator used to disfigure those girls. See here, Mr Riley, it was a wee pair of nail scissors, but here's the thing: when the perp had finished his job, he didn't wipe them clean and what's more, he left his fingerprints all over the wee case they came in.'

'Well, there you have it! If you'd done your job properly before coming round here accusing innocent folk of crimes they didn't commit, then Ricci would be behind bars by now!'

'Sorry to tell you this,' said West, 'but the prints don't belong to Ricci.'

'Well, if it's not him,' said Riley, 'why are you not looking for a match? Why aren't you out looking for him?'

'We are. And guess what? We've found him. They're your prints.'

'I've never heard such garbage!' said Riley as he grabbed another beer. 'Honestly, why on earth... why on earth would I want to hurt those girls?'

'You probably didn't,' said Dougal. 'Not intentionally, anyway. It was Alessandro Ricci you wanted to hurt. Jessica's father...'

Riley froze for a moment, glanced furtively at West, and cracked open the beer.

'...but the reason you wanted to frame him, the real reason, was to get back at Helen for betraying you.'

'Utter tosh!' said Riley. 'Okay, you've outstayed your welcome, pal! I think you'd better leave!'

'So, you followed him. You'd been following him for weeks, you admitted as much yourself. And when you saw Sophie leap from his car outside the club, you went after her. She was already blootered but you probably gave her a wee drink anyway, for shock I imagine. Then you went after Ricci again, you knew where he'd be headed so no rush, eh? But when Jessica jumped out of the car and headed through the park it a was golden opportunity, too good to miss.'

'Dear, dear, dear,' said Riley as he drained the can. 'I despair, I really do. How the hell did you two numpties get to be where you are today? Do you not think the wee lassie would have screamed her head off if I'd been chipping away at her with a pair of scissors?'

'I don't know,' said West. 'Would you? Would you have screamed your head off if you'd had a skinful and then been drugged?'

'Oh, I've heard it all now. You're telling me Jessica was drugged?'

'That's right. You see, Mr Riley, DS McCrae here had a chat with the bloke who stitched you up.'

'Have you been talking to my bookie?'

'Very good,' said Dougal. 'But no. The inspector means the doctor at the hospital. After he'd cleaned you up, he offered you some painkillers and you specifically asked for something strong on account of your low pain threshold. Not only that, you wanted an effervescent.'

'I have trouble swallowing.'

'So he gave you high-dose Co-codamol. Enough for two weeks. And that's what the pathologist found in Jessica's system. Codeine phosphate. That's what knocked her out.'

Riley set the empty can on the table, sat back, and stretched his arms across the top of the sofa.

'I'm an investigative journalist,' he said. 'In many ways my line of work is no different to yours. The difference is, I'm good at it whereas you… Well, I can already see a gaping hole in your theory.'

'Is that so?' said Dougal. 'Do tell.'

'This pair of scissors. And the wee case they came in. Where did you find them? Was it here, in my house?'

'No.'

'Did I leave them in your office?'

'No. Not there either.'

'Then where did you find them?'

'In Helen Sullivan's car,' said Dougal.

'In Helen's car?' said Riley. 'Is that so? And just how do you think they got there?'

'She has a spare key.'

'Aye, exactly! *She* has a spare key. Not me!'

'No, but you know where to find it.'

'So, let me get this straight,' said Riley. 'I broke into Helen's house in the dead of night, took the key, put the scissors in the car, then put the keys back, is that right?'

'Don't be daft,' said Dougal. 'You wouldn't have to.'

'Why not?'

'Because, Mr Riley, when the scenes of crime officers pulled apart her car, they found the spare key. Taped beneath the filler cap. And they also found a lovely thumb print on it. Your thumb print.'

Riley, saying nothing, belched under his breath, bent forward, and pulled on his shoes as West, standing with her hands in her back pockets, smiled at Dougal and nodded.

'Nicholas Riley,' he said, 'I'm arresting you for perverting the course of justice, administering a substance with intent, actual bodily harm, and the murder of Jessica Sullivan. You do not have to say anything but it may harm your defence if you do not mention when questioned something you later rely on in court. Anything you do say may be given in evidence. Do you understand the charge?'

'Grab your coat,' said West. 'You're nicked.'

Epilogue

Apart from the occasional petty and largely inconsequential arguments which revolved mainly around his wife's incessant need to scrub every surface of the house to within an inch of its life, the key to Munro's otherwise faultless and enduring marriage – one that had, until Jean's untimely death, lasted for forty-three years – was a shared passion for sitting in front of a roaring fire with a book in one hand and a whisky in the other whilst trying desperately to stay awake.

However, of the multifarious activities they'd enjoyed together, from pottering around the garden to hiking up the Grey Mare's Tail in a torrential downpour, none could have surpassed the simple pleasure of sharing a meal prepared by her own fair hand.

Recalling with fondness how barely a word was said as they stuffed their faces, he slipped a tray into the oven and uncorked the wine as the door in the hall slammed shut.

'Charlie!' he said. 'I was just about to send for search and rescue. You look happy.'

'I'm delirious. And I'm knackered. And I'm gasping for a drink.'

'I take you've had a good day then?'

'Unbelievable,' said West, beaming as she caught sight of the counter laden with food. 'Blimey, you've pushed the boat out. What's all this, the last supper?'

'It's the last one you'll be getting from me, that's for sure. I've a Camembert in the oven for starters and two steaks ready for the pan.'

'That's not sirloin, is it?'

'Fillet, no less.'

'Pudding?'

'Sticky toffee,' said Munro as he handed her a glass. 'Your very good health.'

'Not on that lot, it won't be.'

'So? What's the story?'

West flung her jacket on the sofa, pulled up a chair and sighed as she took a large sip of wine.

'Where do I begin?' she said. 'John McIver's in the clear but his sidekick, that Isla Thomson woman, she's going down for the murder of Ella MacCall.'

'Is she indeed?'

'Yup, no two ways about it. She's as guilty as sin.'

'How so?'

'Well, you won't believe it, but she and Ella were an item. Thomson was obsessed with her and Ella, poor cow, was driven to depression by her coercive behaviour.'

'That's not right,' said Munro. 'Did she not seek help?'

'She tried, but let's face it, she's a kid, she didn't know where to go so she walked out on Thomson who then succumbed to the old green-eyed monster. She swiped McIver's medication, laced the flask, and gave it to Ella.'

'What is it with folk and relationships these days?' said Munro. 'They dinnae seem cut out for each other.'

'Tell me about it,' said West. 'So, it seems Ella, poor cow, just to get away from Thomson and her mates, went up Goat Fell alone, obviously polished off the soup that Thomson had given her on the way, and that was it, sayonara baby. Oh, and get this, it turns out Nick Riley isn't Jessica's old man after all. It's Alessandro Ricci.'

Munro cocked his head smiled.

'You knew, didn't you?'

'I had my suspicions.'

'How? For crying out loud,' said West, 'how could you have possibly known that?'

'Dear God, Charlie! You've been blessed with the gift of sight, you should learn to use it. Have you not seen Jessica Sullivan? She's more Mona Lisa than Mary Queen of Scots.'

'Well, why didn't you say anything?'

'Because,' said Munro, 'there comes a time when you have to take the stabilisers off the bicycle.'

'Whatever that means.'

'So, that's Ricci off the hook, I assume?'

'Not quite,' said West. 'He'll still do time on the insurance gig because he can't afford to pay the fine, oh, and at the risk of inflating your ego even more, you'll be pleased to know you were right about Helen Sullivan too. It was her who attacked Riley.'

Munro checked the oven, topped up the glasses, and joined West at the table.

'So,' he said, 'that just leaves Jessica and young Sophie.'

'Sorted,' said West, 'but if it wasn't for Dougal then I have to admit I'd probably still be scratching my head.'

'How so?'

'Nick Riley. He's the one who topped Jessica.'

'Well, I thought there was something fishy about the fellow,' said Munro, 'but I didnae see that coming.'

'He was out to frame Ricci for having a ding-dong with his fiancée years ago but he went a bit too far. If he's lucky he might get off with manslaughter, that's if his brief can convince a jury that he didn't mean to do it. Either way, he won't be writing any more articles for a while.'

Munro leaned back and raised his glass.

'To you,' he said. 'Well done, Charlie.'

'Thanks. It's funny really.'

'What is?'

'I was just thinking,' said West. 'All the time I was in London, I spent almost every day taking crap from all the blokes I worked with. The snide comments, the way they'd set me up for a fall, how they did their best to make me look like an idiot. They were convinced I'd never make it. Or rather, they didn't *want* me to make it.'

'You'd be wise to remember, Charlie, it's the cock that crows but it's the hen that delivers the goods.'

'You're a one-off, you know that?' said West nodding towards the oven. 'How long's that going to take?'

'Ten minutes.'

'So, what happened to you earlier? Sloping off on the quiet? What was this secret appointment you had to keep?'

'Och, nothing secret about it,' said Munro. 'I had to get my sodium levels checked.'

'Sodium? What's that about then?'

'I've no idea.'

'Probably too much salt in your diet. Hold on a minute! You can't stand doctors! What's going on?'

'Nothing.'

'If you're keeping something from me...'

'I've nothing to hide.'

'If you say so,' said West, 'but you'd better not be lying. So, what's the plan for tomorrow? Are you heading back to yours to finish your decorating?'

'Not immediately, Charlie, no.'

'In that case, after I've had a good, long lie-in, I'll do us a fry-up, it'll set you up for the day.'

'Not for me, lassie,' said Munro as he laid the table. 'I'm away to Glasgow first thing.'

'Glasgow? What for?'

'Bypass.'

'You're going to Glasgow to look at the bypass?'

'No, no. To have a bypass,' said Munro. 'I'm going into hospital.'

West, already bruised and battered by the day's events, felt as though she'd taken a sucker punch to the jaw.

'You're having a heart bypass?' she said.

'Not one, Charlie. Three.'

'A triple bypass?'

'You know me. I'm not one to do things by halves.'

Still reeling, West stumbled to her feet, snatched the Balvenie from the cupboard, and poured herself a large dram.

'When I came through the door,' she said, 'I really felt like celebrating, but now…'

'And so you should,' said Munro. 'Now calm yourself or you'll ruin your appetite.'

'But it's so unfair! I mean, why? How come you have to go through that when the likes of Riley and…'

'Wheesht, lassie! You're not helping matters by getting upset! Now just you listen to me, it doesnae matter about Riley, or any other murdering lowlife, all you have to remember is that when the game's over, the pawn and the king go back in the same box. Do you get me?'

'I don't know how you can be so relaxed about it, I really don't. So, come on then, what brought this on? Have you had a heart attack or something? I mean, I know you've not been feeling yourself recently but this…'

'Aye, you're not wrong there,' said Munro. 'Truth is, Charlie, I've not been feeling myself for a while; difficulty breathing, cannae make the stairs like I used to, sweating for no good reason. I knew something was wrong so I bit the bullet and got myself checked out.'

'And?'

'Cholesterol. I'd be in better shape if I'd been smoking twenty a day for the last fifty years. The bottom line is, they gave me two options; do nothing and keel over without warning, or take the operation and get another ten, twenty years, maybe.'

'So, it's a no brainer,' said West. 'You're having the op.'

'Of course I am. I'm not ready to slip this mortal coil, lassie. Not just yet.'

'But a heart op! I mean that's serious!'

'Och, it's no different to changing the fuel pump on that Defender of yours!'

'God almighty! Sometimes you're so flipping flippant about everything, it winds me up! So, what happens? Have they talked you through the procedure?'

'They have indeed,' said Munro, 'and if the anaesthetist does his job properly and doesnae finish me off before they start, then I'm in with a shout.'

'Is it dangerous?'

'It's one of the safest procedures around, Charlie. A ninety-five percent success rate.'

'It's the five percent that worries me.'

'I admire your confidence.'

'So how long does it take?'

'Oh, six hours, seven maybe. Could be eight.'

'Eight!' said West. 'Eight hours under the knife! Bloody hell, I don't think I could take that.'

'You don't have to.'

'I bloody well do. Hang on, should you be eating all this if you're having surgery tomorrow?'

'Probably not,' said Munro, 'but they're doing my heart lassie, not my belly and I'm not meeting Saint Peter on an empty stomach.'

'Well, who's taking you?'

'No-one of course. I'll take myself.'

'You will not! I'll do it. And I'll wait until you're done.'

'Don't be daft,' said Munro. 'You'll just be hanging around, getting yourself in a tizz over nothing.'

'Shut it. No arguments, I'm coming with you. Cheese is ready.'

Unable to recall the last time he'd been reprimanded by anyone other than his wife, Munro – tickled by West's forthright if not blatantly disrespectful tone – grinned as he slid a sloppy Camembert onto a plate, fired up the steaks, and returned to his seat.

'There's something else,' he said as he retrieved a small, drawstring pouch from his breast pocket. 'I'd like you to hang on to this for me, just in case.'

'What is it?'

'It's Jean's wedding ring. You can give it back when I get out.'

Struggling to keep her emotions in check, West smiled as she admired the simple, single emerald set in a silver band, and looked earnestly at Munro.

'Are you scared?' she said.

'Och, Charlie, I'll be unconscious when they slice open my legs to pillage a few veins. I'll be unconscious when they crack open my ribs to get to my heart. And I'll still be unconscious when they hack off the blocked bits and replace them with the new, so to answer your question: am I scared?'

Munro drained his glass and winked.

'I'm not scared, lassie. I'm petrified. Aye, that's the word. Petrified.'

Character List

JAMES MUNRO (RETIRED) – Unable to relinquish his duties as a DI, the irrepressible James Munro uses his invaluable experience to trace a missing girl and unwittingly becomes embroiled in the hunt for a double-murderer.

DI CHARLOTTE WEST – Leading the investigation into a murder on the Isle of Arran, West, when left to her own devices, experiences a surge in confidence which has the local constabulary quaking in their boots.

DS DOUGAL McCRAE – Relishing his role as a DS, Dougal, though happiest behind a computer screen, discovers a hitherto unseen side to his personality and shows no mercy when confronting a suspect.

DC DUNCAN REID – Having proved that his maverick approach to policing can get results, DC Reid – given a free rein by West – embraces the opportunity to prove himself further, as long as it doesn't involve travelling by ferry.

DCI GEORGE ELLIOT – The ebullient DCI Elliot, countering the stress caused by staff cuts and under-funding by indulging in his wife's cooking, is ready to help Munro whatever the reason.

ALESSANDRO RICCI – A suave, sophisticated Italian with an eye for the girls leaves his native Tuscany under a cloud, but does his arrival in Ayrshire spell trouble for some of the locals?

HELEN SULLIVAN – A single mother in a dead-end job is swept off her feet when a wealthy stranger arrives in town but her delight is soon overshadowed by the disappearance of her daughter.

NICK RILEY – A jobbing journalist with a nose for trouble is rubbing somebody up the wrong way and soon realises he's made a mistake when the tables are turned.

JOHN McIVER – A burly, benevolent mechanic and leader of the mountain rescue team becomes both angry and confused when accusations of his involvement in a murder begin to fly around the island.

ISLA THOMSON – PE Teacher, fitness freak, and a member of the mountain rescue team, Isla is respected not so much for her selfless role under John McIver, but for her ability to beat any man at arm wrestling in the local pub.

PC BOBBY MACKENZIE – As an islander born and bred, Mackenzie is happy at having to deal with nothing more than the occasional drunk, a lost tourist, or a stolen car, until he meets DI West and sets his sights a wee bit higher.

DR ANDY MCLEOD – The hulking Andy McLeod, happiest in the company of a cadaver with no known cause of death, continues to pursue DI West in the hope of spending his downtime with someone who has a pulse.

If you enjoyed this book, please let others know by leaving a quick review on Amazon. Also, if you spot anything untoward in the paperback, get in touch. We strive for the best quality and appreciate reader feedback.

editor@thebookfolks.com

www.thebookfolks.com

ALSO BY PETE BRASSETT

In this series:

Other titles:

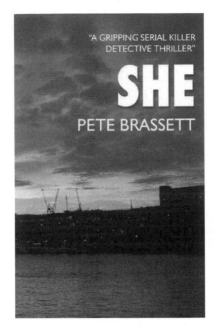

SHE

PETE BRASSETT

SHE

With a serial killer on their hands, Scottish detective
Munro and rookie sergeant West must act fast to trace a
woman placed at the scene of crime. Yet discovering her
true identity, let alone finding her, proves difficult. Soon
they realise the crime is far graver than either of them
could have imagined.

AVARICE

A sleepy Scottish town, a murder in a glen. The local
police chief doesn't want a fuss and calls in DI Munro to
lead the investigation. But Munro is a stickler for
procedure, and his sidekick Charlie West has a nose for a
cover up. Someone in the town is guilty, will they find out
who?

ENMITY

When it comes to frustrating a criminal investigation, this
killer has all the moves. A spate of murders is causing
havoc among in a remote Scottish town. Enter Detective
Inspector Munro to catch the red herrings and uncover an
elaborate and wicked ruse.

DUPLICITY

When a foreign worker casually admits to the murder of a
local businessman, detectives in a small Scottish town
guess that the victim's violent death points to a more
complex cause. Money appears to be a motive, but will
anyone believe that they might be in fact dealing with a
crime of passion?

TERMINUS

Avid fans of Scottish detective James Munro will be
worrying it is the end of the line for their favourite sleuth
when, battered and bruised following a hit and run, the
veteran crime-solver can't pin down a likely suspect.

TALION

A boy finds a man's body on a beach. Police quickly
suspect foul play when they discover he was part of a local
drugs ring. With no shortage of suspects, they have a job
pinning anyone down. But when links to a local business
are discovered, it seems the detectives may have stumbled
upon a much bigger crime than they could have imagined.

PERDITION

A man is found dead in his car. A goat is killed with a
crossbow. What connects these events in a rural Scottish
backwater? DI Charlotte West investigates in this gripping
murder mystery that ends with a sucker punch of a twist.

PENITENT

A missing pensioner. A boxer who keeps getting beat. A woman found dead in the municipal pool. DI Charlie West is charged with finding the connection between these events. As she investigates, the shady past of a small town and a legacy of regret and resentment surfaces.

For more great books, visit: www.thebookfolks.com

52190534R00130

Made in the USA
Middletown, DE
08 July 2019